Slickensides

JOHN BUXTON HILTON

Slickensides

A Derbyshire mystery

St. Martin's Press
New York

Library of Congress Cataloging-in-Publication Data

Hilton, John Buxton.
    Slickensides : a Derbyshire mystery.

    I. Title.
PR6058.I5S55   1987   823′.914   87-16377
ISBN 0-312-01091-5

First published in Great Britain by William Collins Sons & Co., Ltd.

First U.S. Edition

10 9 8 7 6 5 4 3 2 1

Slickensides

CHAPTER 1

On a dry but blustery March day in 1903 three ruggedly healthy boys were heaving at a boulder at the bottom of a hollow in an unarable field in Derbyshire's Upper Dove Valley. All three of them had taken trouble to conceal where they were coming, but it is an understatement to say that hills have eyes: it has sometimes appeared to travellers that these hills must have a tongue as well, so quickly does news of people's doings travel.

The three boys had not yet developed full adult mastery of the art of moving discreetly about the countryside, but it was duly reported in local conclaves that evening that they had tried hard. They had avoided skylines. They had loped fast and silently, sometimes bent almost double to take the fullest advantage of such lips of dead ground as served their purpose. It was even passed on in the bar of the Pig o' Lead—before Septimus Durden came in—that they had all three of them left their homes furtively, as if it would be fatal to be waylaid and asked where they were going.

Humphrey Durden, for example, left the farm called Slickensides over a wall hidden from the house by the angle of a stable and made his way to the field called Middle Furlong by a route that added half an hour to his walking time.

Even Barnard Brittlebank did not leave Walderslow Hall by the drive, but climbed out of the grounds from somewhere among the congeries of outhouses behind the big house. But he was not unobserved. The pale face of a woman of indeterminate age was watching him from an upstairs window in the west wing, and she followed his progress until he frustrated her by disappearing over a crest. At that crucial moment he looked back to let her know that he was aware of her unwanted vigilance. Barnard Brittlebank could interpret the look on her face, but the village did not know what to make of Miss Machin.

The third boy had greater difficulty than the others in evading his family. He was due that day for a fitting for his first young man's suit, and his parents had arranged to take him to Buxton by train from Parsley Hay for an appointment with his tailor. William Cartledge escaped only by downright deception, feigning an attack of diarrhœa so virulent that it was unsafe for him to move more than a few yards away from a haven. It was remarkable how quickly he recovered after his parents had departed for their Saturday shopping. (This information was duly relayed to the Pig o' Lead not by any whispering in the hills, but by Jobie Bellis, who had spent the day at the Cartledges' doing an outside painting job.)

When the boys came together at the hollow in Middle Furlong, any observer could have seen that although they had met for a common purpose, they were not friends. As one of the astute minds in the Pig o' Lead said, it was only because of the difficulty of shifting that boulder that they had had to team up. But there was no agreement among them about the best way of doing it: lain where it had for millennia, that stone resisted change.

The three did not even look as if they all came from the same human tribe. Humphrey Durden was seventeen. He had left school five years ago and was wearing scuffed moleskin trousers, a cast-off jacket of his father's, and sundry garments of unimaginable provenance. William Cartledge was of the same age, but more cleanly dressed, albeit in clothes that had been superannuated from appearances in public. His cuffs ended ludicrously far above his wrists and the gaps between his boots and the bottoms of his trousers distinctly evoked the country yokel: a label which the Cartledges would strenuously have resisted. He travelled daily to Buxton to attend a school that had been endowed in the reign of Charles II.

The third boy, Barnard Brittlebank, had equipped himself with a blue boiler suit for the occasion. This working-man's attire, still something of an innovation in the first decade of the century, was the newest and most unspoiled rig of the trio. Although he was three years younger than the other two, he appeared to assume leadership by right, though his command was not always accepted without argument: the other two did not jump about on his orders, and from time to time he appeared to be having to harangue them.

But when their first labour was complete, and the large stone had been levered aside from whatever it was covering, it was clear that the others did not deny his privilege to be the first to lower himself down the narrow and almost vertical shaft that was now exposed. He showed them yet another warrant of his superiority, a brand-new battery-powered hand-lamp, fitted with a shining prismatic reflector. It was common for Barnard Brittlebank to own things that other people had never even heard of. Humphrey Durden was carrying a small sack from which he brought out a round hurricane lantern, but all that William Cartledge had in the way of lighting was a crumpled brown paper bag containing half a dozen candles and a box of vestas.

The hole down which Barnard Brittlebank lowered his legs was neither easy nor comfortable to negotiate. For long seconds his torso remained above ground-level while his feet sought a secure foothold below, and then he had to raise himself a foot or so to free his wedged right arm to manipulate his lamp. Humphrey Durden, broader-built, followed him clumsily, though his movements were in the long run quicker. William Cartledge, the slightest-framed of the three, ought in theory to have had the least physical difficulty, but at the last moment he did not seem enthusiastic. As the top of his head was about to disappear, he shouted something down into the pit, but his words were not audible in the wildness of the outside world, where in spite of the blue sky, a Pennine breeze was setting up a whine among jagged crags.

Mary Ann Durden sat high on the hillside opposite the hollow and did as she had been told: she kept watch. She was wearing a long brown frock of coarse and heavy material, the hem of its skirt somewhere between her ankles and her heels, and she still had on the white pinafore that she wore about the less dirty of her housework—though by now it was rather less than spotless and bore little evidence of the ironing-board. Mary Ann was thirteen, and would be a primitive beauty in a very few years' time. But as yet her frame still had to fill out, her long black hair still looked girlish and her lean legs were not yet those of a woman. Despite her conscious efforts to make a proper job of what they had told her to do, she was shivering—and it was not because of the cold. There was something about the waterswallow in Middle Furlong that always caused the gooseflesh to creep up her thighs and back. They called it a waterswallow, but it was only in freak seasons that it was seen to swallow water. The waterswallow belonged to an age thousands of years before there had been farm buildings at Slickensides. Once, a few years ago, Mary Ann had tried to see past the boulder that the boys had now shifted, and even in that brief moment she had felt as if eyes were watching from somewhere behind her. Today she knew privately that any look-out was futile. What could she do if somebody did come? How would she be able to get down the slope and to the head of the pothole to shout a warning without giving them away? She knew privately too that that was characteristic of boys: if something desirable was impossible, all they had to do was to order someone else to do it. She knew that she was the weakness in the boys' plan —and she suspected that they had conscripted her only so that they could have someone to show off to.

The afternoon was long and slow. A plover wheeled stridently and tirelessly, intent on persuading her that her nest was elsewhere, but otherwise there was no life in Middle Furlong that she could see. Spring was no more than a few days old. There had been no warmth in the year so far, no sap was rising and there were still no new shoots among the dead straggle of last year's grasses.

She had no way of telling what was happening down the waterswallow. To her eyes there was an almost human cruelty about the gash at the bottom of the hollow. It looked utterly deserted—there was nothing to suggest that her brother and two other boys had gone down there an hour ago. She wanted to climb down and peer into the shaft where the boulder had lain—but they had expressly forbidden her to do that. Then she saw that someone else had come into the field. Miss Machin had climbed the stile at the lower end: a strange woman, about whom there were all manner of rumours in Walderslow, none of them proven—and none of them charitable. She had been Barnard Brittlebank's nurse, then governess, and her position at the Hall nowadays was a fruitful subject for day-to-day, month-to-month specu- lation in the village. Some spoke as if she were the brains and power behind the Brittlebanks, others said that she was nothing more than an underpaid drudge incapable of speaking up for herself. She was a small woman, not well fleshed out and of little visible feminine charm, and the look in her eyes said that she knew the answers to questions that ordinary people did not begin to understand. What was more, that look carried the strong suggestion that any such answer was always likely to be both forceful and disagree- able. Miss Machin was someone whom Walderslow con- sidered it safest to avoid.

She came now, despite the sear grasses dragging about her skirts and the earth soiling her elastic-sided boots, with wilful strides towards the waterswallow. She stooped over the hole where the boulder had lain, cupped her hands and shouted down it something that Mary Ann could not hear. The irregular rim of the gap was scarcely more than a yard across and its angle of descent was not plumb vertical. Knobs and spurs of rock jutted out at either side, and these had been the first obstacles that the boys had had to negotiate. And these hindrances also prevented anyone from seeing more than the first few feet down the swallow. Mary Ann remembered the unhealthy smell of damp earth and decay down there. But if Miss Machin had any feeling that unseen eyes were watching her, she seemed in no way put out by it. She was afraid, but it was of something more concrete than phantom watchers. Mary Ann knew intuitively that she feared for the physical safety of a boy who was too big to be harassed in front of his friends by such spinsterish concern.

The plover was incensed into a fresh bout of shrieking circles. The wind whined up a side-clough with the effect of an organ-pipe. Charlotte Machin bent and shouted again. Only when there was still no response did she turn about and look all round her. She did not see Mary Ann, and the girl kept perfectly still.

Then a head, followed by shoulders, pulled itself painfully out of the hole. It was William Cartledge. He had drawn himself out as far as his waist when Miss Machin turned back and saw him. His appearance so startled her that even from her distance Mary Ann saw her jump and heard a little squeal as she threw up her hand to her mouth.

Then it became agonizingly impossible to tell what was happening. Miss Machin asked William Cartledge something and he replied. Then he lowered himself feet first back the way he had come. From time to time Miss Machin shouted down the hole, but the wind always seemed to rise to a crescendo just as Mary Ann thought she had caught a phrase.

Another full hour passed. The shadow of Middle Furlong's tallest and most grotesque outcrop had begun to lengthen over the grass by the time William Cartledge came up again. The greenery was already losing colour in the failing light and a couple of Septimus Durden's sheep, up on the highest ridge, had begun to crop hungrily, as if they knew that the time left for eating was short. William Cartledge crawled out and stood in the hollow with his limbs free. His body was shaking, his shoulders were rounded, and he had obviously undergone an experience that he would not care to repeat. He kept plucking at his clothes as if they were soaked through and clinging to his skin.

Barnard Brittlebank emerged a minute or two later. He was in firmer command of himself than William, and apparently in voluble mood. But Miss Machin became voluble too. She gestured angrily to him, evidently establishing that she was now in command. Very shortly after that, the three of them set out, openly and with no attempt to conceal themselves, in the direction of Slickensides Farm. It was now clear to Mary Ann that her brother was not going to come up out of the hole. Would she ever see him again?

The afternoon's goings-on had only been possible because today was Saturday. On Saturdays at midday Septimus Durden drank deeply in the Pig o' Lead and came home fit only to fall asleep the moment he had eaten his dinner. The family were supposed to get on with their work about house and farm as usual, but even their mother took advantage of Saturdays.

No one ever spoke directly to Mary Ann about what had happened that day. She was left to put it together for herself as best she could. It was late in the evening that Humphrey was carried back into the house, evidently very badly hurt. But it was not because he had exposed himself to danger that their father was angry with him, not because he had been deceitful and had deserted his work, though those things were bad enough. There was something secret, something worse than any of this. What was unforgivable, Mary Ann gathered, was that he had taken strangers down the waterswallow, had let them see things that only the Durdens had the right to know about.

His father could not thrash him, because his back was so badly hurt, but he promised him that he would deal out punishment as soon as he was sufficiently recovered. It was not until the end of the first week in April, a fortnight later, that the thrashing took place, the pair of them locked in the dairy. It took Humphrey an hour to get over it, lying in the empty pig-trough in the yard where his father threw him. The flogging was the only talking-point in the Pig o' Lead that night—until Septimus Durden came in.

CHAPTER 2

Eight years later, on a November evening in 1911, two men turned their cheeks from the buffeting of the elements as they crossed from Buxton's Midland Station to the Ashbourne line. To make their discomfort worse, they had no time to snatch a meal before catching their connection. And the whipcord wind that lashed their faces promised a foul night—likely to be fouler still in the higher reaches to which they were travelling.

One of them was tall, lean, clean-shaven, ascetic-looking and sinewy. The other was shorter, broader across the shoulders, and occasionally patted a military moustache. A porter carried their bags over to the L & NW platform and they tried to question him about the relative advantages of their two possible destinations. The porter, a jealous-minded local patriot, faithfully expounded the virtues of both places, but declined to state an overriding case for either of them. The argument was still going on when the ticket inspector visited them in their First Class compartment. (All the way from London to Buxton they had travelled Third.)

'Hurdlow is nearer to our inn by a couple of miles,' the

tall, lean man was saying, 'and that will make a difference if we have to cover the stretch on foot. Parsley Hay, on the other hand, appears to lie at the junction of two railway companies. It should therefore be a more ambitious settlement, with a better chance of our hiring a conveyance at this hour of night.'

Soon there was pitch blackness on either side of them. Through the unclean carriage window they could see their dim lights undulating over the rough-hewn limestone of deep cuttings. The tall man lifted his valise from the rack, unstrapped it and brought out a deerstalker hat and an amber-stemmed calabash pipe, which he drew from its lambskin case with loving care.

'Don't forget, Doctor—from now on you walk with a stiff leg.'

'If there's no cab to be had, I'll be doing that soon enough.'

There was no cab at Parsley Hay. The station was a junction—in the history of rural railways even an historic one, but there was in fact only the most rudimentary of settlements to be discovered there. The only official on duty at the confluence of the London and North Western and the former Cromford and High Peak line was a misanthropic all-purpose porter who could not wait to lock his doors and put out his oil-lamps.

'Cab? Where do you think this is? London Road, Manchester?'

The darkness was all but absolute. Even when they came within sight of the lights of Monyash, it looked as if the inhabitants of the ancient lead-mining village were conducting a communal drive against candle-consumption. The cut-throat wind that was whistling over from the tumuli of Cales Dale and Long Rake made a nonsense of London cloaks and capes.

'Jesus Christ!' swore the man whom the other had referred to as *Doctor*. 'Is it worth it?'

'Believe me, my friend, our earnings will be worth a long and well-found winter on the coast of southern France. We need all the funds we can raise if my new system is to have a fair chance at the tables. I also suspect that it is going to be our most stimulating case since the affair of the speckled band.'

'Speckled band?'

'You remember nothing I tell you, do you? You're going to let me down,' the tall man said. 'I cannot persuade you to absorb anything, can I?'

It took the pair an hour and a half to reach the Pig o' Lead at Walderslow, where they had rooms booked—if, as looked doubtful, His Majesty's mails penetrated into such regions. Their reception at the inn was mixed. Joe Bramwell, the landlord, fussed round them, as if he believed himself reflected in some sort of glory from the characters that they appeared to be. He led them upstairs, showed them their rooms, did his best to answer their flood of questions and let drop various things about himself that he considered impressive.

Down in the bar the conversation was speculative and uninformed. Some of the villagers had heard speak of Sherlock Holmes. It was even possible that one or the other of them had read some of the stories. And there were clearly a few present who thought that the Baker Street detective was a genuine and living character.

'Is it you who's sent for him, then, Septimus?'

'Nay—I couldn't afford the sort of fee he'd be asking,' Septimus Durden said. 'In any case, our friend the Inspector here has been taking measurements up and down my yard all afternoon.'

He indicated a mournful-looking gentleman who was sipping brandy and warm water in a corner a little removed from the rest of them. Men said it would not be many years before Inspector Brunt was compulsorily retired. A lifetime of High Peak weathering had imprinted enduring fatigue in a face crowded with bumps, wens and moles. He was for ever using his handkerchief to pat his permanently watery eyes.

'Wait till they come down again,' a man called Broomhead said. 'We'll string them on a bit—see what they're really made of.'

But there was no immediate outbreak of talk when Joe brought the couple back downstairs. He served them cold roast beef, pickles and ale and for a while a subdued and shy silence fell over the company. It was the man who wanted to be taken for Holmes who finally broke it.

'So, gentlemen—I find myself in Walderslow. What can you tell me about Walderslow?'

This was too generalized a question for the men who lived there. Somebody muttered something about it not being a bad old place, but the entity and purpose of their village against the background of the cosmos were things they were not accustomed to put into words. They were inclined to take Walderslow for granted.

'Nay—it's tha who ought to be telling us about ourselves,' Ned Broomhead said. 'If tha'rt who tha looks to be, I shouldna think there's many of us can hang on to many secrets while th'art about.'

'That's true,' the stranger said. 'Every object in this room has its history written large about it.'

He rose, crossed the room with a fit man's strides, and picked up a plain, gun-metal vesta-box that was lying on the table in front of Septimus Durden.

'You, sir, I am sure, will have no objection if I use this article to demonstrate what can be achieved by the science of deductive logic.'

He carried the thing over and examined it at various professional-looking angles under the Pig o' Lead's most effective hanging oil-lamp. He tapped the box, smelled at it, wiped something off it with his fingertip and tasted it, brought out a hand-lens and examined it obliquely. Then he looked at old Septimus with respectful curiosity.

'May I assume that you spend a great deal of your time handling cheese, sir?'

There was a gentle murmur of admiration.

'And if I may say so, a somewhat unusual cheese,' the stranger said. 'A cheese with a certain bouquet. A nobleman among cheeses.'

'Aye—Slickensides,' somebody muttered.

'I also discern that you are occasionally in the habit of carrying a ferret about in your jacket pocket, that your favourite tobacco is an aromatic twist, that you used to brew your own beer, but that you gave up doing that some years ago.'

'Good old Slickensides!' somebody else said. 'It used to make us fart like barge-horses.'

'Truly remarkable,' said the man posing as Watson, and old Septimus was looking at the amateur detective with his lower jaw loosely fallen.

'Happen tha could let us into a few of thy secrets, Mr Holmes,' he said.

'A series of commonplaces, really,' said the austere visitor. 'Though I say it myself, my olfactory discrimination has become highly developed over the years, and there is a patina over the surface of your vesta-box that quickly yielded up to me its legend of cheese and tobacco. As for your brewing, I had no difficulty in detecting a distinct odour of wort—an extract of malt of a mature, not to say ancient character. From this I deduce that it is a very long time indeed since you have handled a brewing vat. As for the ferret, I observe that a minute hair has become in some way caught up in the hinged lid of your little box. I might add that a decade or so ago I published a modest little monograph on the summer and winter coats of domesticated and semi-domesticated mammals.'

During this display, some of the drinkers had cast coy sideways glances in the direction of Inspector Brunt, wondering what might be his professional reaction to this virtuosity. Brunt, regarding the stranger as though through a film of tears, wriggled his body in his seat and brought something out of an inside pocket.

'I dare say, sir, that you have already inferred that I am a professional policeman—an inspector from the detective department of the county force. Or perhaps our landlord has told you about me—as you obviously got him to prime you about Septimus Durden and his vesta-box while he was showing you your room. I would greatly appreciate anything you can in your wisdom tell me about the owner of these.'

And he handed the visitor a pair of spectacles in a cheap case, so old that they were almost an antique, made of unpolished nickel, and with narrow, oval eye-pieces that obviously catered for someone very short-sighted indeed.

'Holmes' examined them carefully.

'I would say they belong to someone who will not see three score years and ten again,' he said.

'A man, or a woman?' Brunt asked, quietly and incisively.

'Holmes' gave this thought.

'Oh, a man for certain. In the age in which we live, I am sure that any lady would wish to wear something at least a trifle more elegant.'

'Would you like to speculate on the profession of the gentleman concerned?'

'They obviously belong to someone much addicted to reading.'

'Yes—but some people read as a mere pastime. I wonder if you see anything there that might suggest the man's vocation?'

'From their style—or rather, from their lack of style—I would say that they belong to a scrivener, rather than to his master. A lawyer's clerk, perhaps—or some toiler in a counting-house.'

The company were now listening in a silence such as they had not accorded to the stranger's demonstration. They had recognized—though perhaps they were not familiar with the phrase—the *Greek meets Greek* syndrome. The man was becoming increasingly reluctant to reply and Brunt was clearly going to persist until he had forced him to commit himself. It was notorious that Brunt was nothing if not a persister.

'I believe that the real Sherlock Holmes could have looked at them and told us the man's height,' Brunt said.

'Yes, well, there must obviously be a correlation between the length of their arms and the physique of their wearer. I see these belonging to a man between five feet nine inches and six feet tall.'

'Are there any traces of domesticated or semi-domesticated fur caught in the frame? Do you think he keeps ferrets in his hair?'

'You will have your little joke, Inspector. But this is a scientific exercise—'

'At least you might tell us whether he is a careless man or a man of fastidious habits.'

'He is obviously a careful man. There are no scratches or other signs of ill-handling, and the lenses are reasonably clean even though they have been in your pocket.'

'What about his ears? They have obviously been in close contact with his ears. Can you describe the man's ears to us?'

'He has rather a large head.'

'In point of fact *she* has a very small head—a very small head indeed,' Brunt said. 'She is a very careless and untidy woman—otherwise she would not have lost her glasses—and she is still at least fifteen years short of her three score years and ten. She is barely five feet tall and she left these behind when she was decorating the church with flowers for last Sunday's services. They were handed to me, and I have brought them to see if anyone here will be passing her cottage on their way home. Although still in early middle age, she is generally known as Old Mother Mycock.'

Laughter all round—and evaporation of any sympathy that might at first have accumulated in the stranger's favour. There were men here who had reason to be wary of Tom Brunt—but when Londoners were present, they were proud of him as a home product.

'Old Mother Mycock is illiterate. You must forgive us if those of us who know her are amused at the image of her serving in a solicitor's office or counting-house.'

'You must understand, Inspector Brunt—'

'That you are not Sherlock Holmes.'

'Indeed, sir—how could I be? That gentleman is a fiction —the felicitous invention of Sir Arthur Conan Doyle.'

'I'm glad to hear you admit it.'

'On the other hand, sir—'

'Holmes' handed Brunt a visiting card, at the same time publicly announcing his identity.

'Mr Harvey Harlow—and my colleague, Dr Thomas Topliss—at your service, gentlemen.'

He did not specify what services of his he thought they might need. Brunt put the visiting card away in his wallet with a professional air that looked for a moment little short of sinister. He gave the impression that he was glad to have it in his possession—and that he would be coming back to it later.

'And may I say, sir,' Harvey Harlow continued, 'that I am in regular correspondence with Sir Arthur. I would not flatter myself that his most successful literary creation is entirely based upon the exploits of my medical friend and myself, but the fact remains that I do keep the eminent author informed from time to time of our more striking achievements in the field of private detection. The affair of the dancing men, for example, which purports to have taken place at a manor house in the county of Norfolk, has remarkable similarities with a case which the doctor and I actually handled on the Dorsetshire coast. And the case of the speckled band—'

'I do not doubt that you are in correspondence with Sir Arthur,' Brunt said. 'Whether Sir Arthur has ever considered it worth his while to reply to you is, I suggest, a separate question.

Brunt stood up, finished his drink and buttoned his overcoat. A more discriminating public than that of the Pig o' Lead might have been sensitive to the fact that their local thief-taker was not sartorially vain. The buttons of his outer garment did not match each other, and none of them matched the coat, but this did not seem to affect anyone's attitude to him. Knees were moved aside to allow him passage across the bar and the man nearest the outside door went so far as to rise from his seat and open it for him. Mr Harvey Harlow made haste to follow him out. They stood and looked at each other on the doorstep of the inn, illuminated only by such light as escaped from its ill-fitting curtains.

'You appeared just now to have been declaring yourself hostile to my implied offer of gratuitous assistance, Inspector Brunt.'

'I, hostile?'

'Perhaps you should know that a London police officer, whom for obvious reasons I would rather not name, but who is the prototype of Sir Arthur's Inspector Lestrade—'

'Come off it!' Brunt said.

'Have it your own way. But there are detectives in the capital who have been glad to have me on hand in the background.'

'We are not in the capital,' Brunt said.

'But I am surely correct in assuming that your reason and mine for being among this concertingly eccentric community this evening boil down to the same purpose. Not to put too fine a point on it, Inspector, we are working on the same case.'

'Indeed?' Brunt said. 'And what case is that, may I ask outright?'

'I am here to investigate the unaccountable disappearance of Mr Barnard Brittlebank,' Harlow said portentously.

'And may I ask at whose instigation you are here?'

'You must know that it would go against all codes of professional etiquette for me to reveal that.'

'And it would be just as unprofessional of me to share any of my findings with you.'

Harvey Harlow was too experienced to play into Brunt's hands by losing his temper. He even went so far as to control his frigid pomposity.

'At least I am sure there is nothing in the standing orders of your force that forbids you to clear up a purely etymological difficulty for a passing stranger.'

'If I knew what you were talking about, I would do my best to help you over any non-confidential hurdle,' Brunt said.

'During the last half-hour I have heard a particular word some six or seven times, and each time it has had a different meaning.'

Brunt looked at him questioningly.

'Slickensides,' Harlow said. 'In one breath it appears to be the name of a farmhouse, in the next a brand of cheese —and two minutes later it seems to refer to beer.'

'Elementary, my dear Harlow. Slickensides is all of those things. It is the name of a cheese that is made at a farm. Although only produced in small commercial quantities, it is much sought after by connoisseurs and even has a few regular customers on the mainland of Europe. Its qualities are said to derive in part from the spores of certain fungi which flourish in the air of the cave-mouth in which the cheeses are stored to mature. Slickensides is also the name of a beer which Mr Septimus Durden used to brew on his premises—a fermentation of mythological potency.'

'And does he no longer brew it?'

'He gave up some seven years ago, on the ultimate insistence of his wife, for reasons directly related to that potency.

And I predict that you will not have been in Walderslow very much longer, Mr Harlow, before you encounter yet another meaning of the same word. Slickensides was also the name of a lead-mine before the farmhouse was built. In fact the dairy of Slickensides the farm was once the *coe*, that is the local word for a storehouse, built over the main shaft of Slickensides the mine. As often happened when a miner drove his adit into one of these hillsides, he stuck his pick through to a natural system of chambers and galleries.'

'How interesting! *Slickensides* is, I take it, essentially a dialect word?'

'Far from it. It is an orthodox geological term, used regularly by specialists and scholars. Slickensides is the name given to the highly polished, highly compressed surface of spar and metallic ore which was produced when two rock-faces slid against each other during the formation of a fault. You must understand that when this happened, millions of years ago, the pressure of mighty moving hillsides on the strata was immense. When that energy is trapped behind a rock-face, the result is called slickensides.'

'You fascinate me,' Harvey Harlow said.

Brunt was unaffected by urbane sarcasm. He went on as if uninterrupted.

'One of the results of this immense primeval pressure is that slickensides can be dangerously explosive. Miners are known to have been killed when the tip of their pick has released this ancient compression of energy.'

'And are these mines still being worked, Inspector?'

'Very few of them nowadays. Veins have run out and hundreds of thousands of gallons of water have run in. And royalties payable to landowners and the Crown have proved prohibitive.'

Brunt was about to walk away into the night, but he had an afterthought.

'The power pent up behind slickensides, Mr Harlow, has

been there since before man walked this landscape. This is a neighbourhood with a jealous and explosive history. You would be well advised to look carefully wherever you are thinking of striking with your pick. A careless blow could release God knows what. And that applies to other things, besides rock-faces.'

Brunt walked briskly away, in spite of the darkness—a man who knew exactly where he was going and how to get there. Mr Harvey Harlow turned and went back into the inn, where for the next hour he and Dr Topliss were kept safely amused with local legends, most of them centring on Septimus Durden, a man no older than his fifties, who nevertheless radiated something of the aura of a patriarch, albeit a somewhat wizened one. Nothing about Septimus Durden appeared to be normal or average. His cheese found its way to the tables of Parisian gourmets and in its vintage years his beer had on occasion been known to put almost the entire male community of Walderslow into a temporary coma. Durden's own capacity for it had been significant, and as he now had to make do with a commercial product, so had his consumption increased in inverse proportion to its lethal potential.

It soon became clear, however, that Septimus Durden's deportment depended very closely on the will and whimsy of his wife, who emerged from the evening's repertoire as a subject of universal awe. What she could not achieve by the cutting edge of her tongue, Ellen Durden accomplished by other strokes of genius. There was the story of how one night the company had been disturbed by a rattling of old metal in the porch of the inn. When somebody opened the door, Mrs Durden was in the act of trundling in an old iron bedstead.

'I thought perhaps he was making his home here, and he'd be more comfortable if he had this.'

There were many such anecdotes. Did it occur to detective or doctor that this high level of entertainment was diverting

every man present from talking about other things that
might matter more?

Brunt had in the meanwhile made his way to Ted Milward's house, where to Ted's delight he had asked for
lodging for the night.

Ted, who had retired ten years ago, had been Walderslow's constable for more than a quarter of a century.
He was a white-haired, massive man, who had put on weight
since the end of his more active years and who plodded
about his house on feet that seemed to be wearing boots,
even after he had taken them off. Brunt knew that Milward
had the measure at all times of the pulse, respiration and
blood pressure of Walderslow. He was a man who had made
few mistakes in his career, and no bad ones. He had never
acted precipitately in his life and had always used his
own judgement about what and what not to report to his
superiors. As a policeman, he had cared what happened on
his beat—and not infrequently off it as well. He had his
own code of justice, which Walderslow knew about—and
understood.

'So,' Brunt summed up for him. 'We have a couple here
who pretend they're Sherlock Holmeses when they're in the
company of those who know no better—and who have
another likely story up their sleeves for those not taken in
by the first one. And this Mr Harvey Harlow claims that
he is here to investigate the disappearance of Barnard
Brittlebank. It's the first I've heard of that. *Has* Barnard
Brittlebank disappeared?'

'He's gone away, that's all I know. Ten days or so ago a
jobbing carriage from out Longnor way came to fetch him.
But nobody I know has said anything but that he's gone off
in the normal way of his life. And good riddance to him. A
lot of people have the feeling that life may have fewer
unpleasant surprises in store for them, if Barnard
Brittlebank isn't in immediate reach.'

'So if there's anything at all in Harlow's claim, it means

that they don't know at Walderslow Hall where the youngster's gone this time? I can't think that anybody but Horatio
Brittlebank would have set a private detective on the case.'

'Oh, I don't know—'

Ted Milward spoke slowly, as if to stay abreast of his own
thought processes.

'It depends where this Harlow advertises his services.
There's all the difference in the world between those who
read the *Morning Post* and those who take the *Daily Mail*.'

'I don't recall ever having seen Harlow's name in a
newspaper.'

'Neither do I, but I'll take a look into it. I'll go over to
the Reading Room at Hartington in the morning.'

'Who else is likely to have called them in, if not the
Brittlebanks?'

'I don't know—'

Milward had still not come to the end of trying to work
things out.

'If he's gone off without saying where, it might possibly
mean heartbreak for young Mary Ann Durden.'

'There's been something between young Brittlebank and
Mary Ann?'

'Enough to while away an autumn month for Brittlebank
—but I doubt whether that's the way Mary Ann will have
been looking at it. And I can't see either Septimus or Ellen
taking that lying down.'

'It depends how much Mary Ann took lying down,' Brunt
said. 'I thought there was an understanding between her
and William Cartledge?'

'That, too. But I'm afraid young Cartledge has let himself
appear faint-hearted in the eyes of that fair lady.'

'Tomorrow, Ted, I shall be back here not very long
after I've gone away—if you catch what I mean. There's
something here I don't like the look of.'

'You're not thinking it has anything to do with what
you're here for, are you, Tom?'

'Oh, that? Attempted break-in at Septimus's creamery—broken window, and a rough and ready attempt to force the frame, but no sign that anything was actually missing. Some dead-beat seeing a casual chance, from the look of it. The only thing was, the dog was dead. If the dog hadn't been dead, I don't think the Durdens would have called us in. They don't care for us, even when they have a legitimate complaint. But killing a dog is something they wouldn't forgive. In any case, it was Ellen Durden who asked for me to be brought in. I've sent the animal's corpse over to the veterinary surgeon at Ashbourne, so that we can see if she'd been poisoned. If she was, then the thing must have been planned in advance, and it will look a lot worse. I haven't had a case in Walderslow for years, Ted. When I get two together—and a false Sherlock Holmes into the bargain—I'd be slow-witted not to stay in the offing.'

'I'll have my ears on the ground in the morning,' Ted said.

CHAPTER 3

Walderslow was in the habit of waking early, so Brunt did not appear a curiosity by walking to Parsley Hay station—through two farmyards and across four fields—at an hour when city men were still barely conscious of their beckoning counters and desks. He left by the first train, and got off it again five minutes later at Dowlow, thinking nothing of the labour of walking back to where he had come from. He had said to Ted Milward last night that it would be no bad thing to allow Mr Harvey Harlow to believe that as far as detection was concerned he had Walderslow to himself. Ted Milward had promised that he would move in his usual way about the village and pay particular attention to where Harvey Harlow, thus uninhibited, paid his first call. But as it happened, Brunt discovered the answer to this for himself.

As he commonly did on country duty when the fields were dry, he approached his objective across country, and his route took him along the northern edge of Middle Furlong. And there he caught sight of Mary Ann Durden, sitting on the upper slope, opposite the waterswallow, whose boulder had long ago been levered back into position. He could see at first sight—anyone who was not spiritually blind could have seen it—that something had gone radically wrong in the girl's life. The daughters of small farmers on these unproductive holdings were not given to sitting mooning about the fields at this hour of the morning, and *mooning* was the word for Mary Ann. If she had been an aspiring poetess, she could not more effectively have portrayed the torment of *mal de siècle*. Brunt also took note that she had grown into the sort of young woman who could break men's hearts at sight: a woman whose limbs and breasts, even in dejection, openly promised life and love. Even her self-pity could not conceal her Maker's intention for her.

Brunt cast a quick look at the lie of the land to see the quickest way of reaching her. But she was forty feet above him, and having spotted him, was already on the move. She had every advantage: behind her lay square miles of vastness in which she would know her way about every tussock and gully. He abandoned at conception any thought he might have had of giving chase. She vanished behind a low dip on the skyline with the lissome silence of an animal native to the hills.

Brunt had seen many a Derbyshire girl go through what was torturing Mary Ann—and he had no doubt that the same thing happened to young women as they emerged from adolescence in the mill-towns of Lancashire, on the pot-banks of Staffordshire—and even, he supposed, along the more easy-going by-roads of the southern counties. The more constricted their rearing had been, the more wildly did they revolt. The more submissive their thraldom to

church, chapel, village or street, the more savagely defiant
were those who dared to attempt escape. But these were
few, a minority among their generation. For every one who
thought of making a dash for freedom and improvement,
nine were content to let their conventional fate lap over
them. And seldom did the fugitives succeed in going far.
The rabbit who runs from the ferret towards the tempting
circle of sky, as often as not finds her limbs entangled in a
hunter's net.

Brunt watched the girl flee—flee from *him*—and knew
that there went one who had sniffed a spicy air. He made
his way from the waterswallow to the farm and approached
the Slickensides cluster of outhouses from their rear. He had
all but gone past a couple of back-to-back sties, at present
vacant, when he saw, obliquely behind him in one of them,
a young man doing nothing with a fork in his hand. Brunt
knew that he was doing nothing for the adequate reason
that since the place had recently been thoroughly swilled
out, there was nothing in there for him to do.

Humphrey Durden, now 25, was a thickened, knitted-
browed version of the youngster who at 17 had been hurt
at the bottom of the waterswallow—an incident of which
Brunt as yet knew nothing. The injury could not have been
serious in the long term, because there was no sign of any
physical incapacity about him now. He was strong in the
slow-moving way of the labourer who knows that if he
hurries over the job that he is doing, he will be given another
as soon as he has finished. But at the moment he was
motionless, with lowered shoulders, the stance of one who
hoped that the man who was passing would not catch sight
of him. But Brunt stopped and spoke to him over the wall
of the enclosure. Humphrey Durden looked at him with
nothing more complex than the wish that neither of them
were here.

'Is your father in the house?' Brunt asked him.

Durden made a sound that would have been immediately

comprehensible to the usual occupant of his refuge.

'Has anyone else been here this morning?'

Humphrey Durden cleared his throat, the extemporization of one who recognized that here was a question that would have to be answered sooner or later.

'Who?' Brunt asked.

'Them. Them that's staying at the Pig.'

'Been here long, have they?'

Measured parcels of time played little part in Humphrey Durden's existence.

'Came just after the church clock struck half past.'

'And you thought you'd keep out of their way, did you?'

This was more than it was truly fair to ask him. Humphrey Durden glowered as he tried to think of something safe to reply.

'Still in the house with your father and mother, are they?'

Humphrey Durden nodded.

They heard a door open and voices speaking. Brunt, whose movements these days were generally those of a man beginning to be old, stepped with a spurt of unexpected smartness alongside the sties and crossed to the corner of a low-built store, from where he could see what was going on at the front of the farmhouse. Harlow and Topliss had come out and were standing on the doorstep finishing a conversation with Septimus Durden, Harlow's deerstalker and the doctor's greatcoat opulently out of place against the litter of the neglected yard. Words did not carry over the distance, but it was clear that Durden was by no means out of harmony with his visitors. It was apparent that they were talking about the creamery, for all three kept looking towards that building. Then a small wispy-haired and wiry little woman came out of the house. Ellen Durden pushed her way rudely from behind her husband, edging him out of the way with a bucket she was carrying. She seemed to have a contempt for private detectives, no matter in whose image they presented themselves, for she shoved herself unnecessarily between the two London men, and standing less than a couple of feet from them she threw a pailful of predominantly liquid filth across the yard. Harlow had to bring out a large silk handkerchief to wipe droplets from his cheek. Durden swung round to look murderously at his wife, but she was unmoved by his rage and went back into the kitchen as petulantly as she had come out.

The three men then walked across to the creamery, where Brunt saw Harlow go through dramatically impressive motions, bringing out a magnifying glass to examine splinters on the windowsill. Durden was watching eagerly, plainly admiring whatever nonsensical virtuosity Harlow was play-acting now. Then he brought keys out of his waistcoat pocket, opened the several locks that secured the dairy door—a procedure through which Brunt had had to wait patiently yesterday. They all went in and stayed there for some minutes, during which time Ellen Durden came out of the house again.

She crossed the yard and, brisk in her movements, looked in at a number of doors in succession. Then she stood in the middle of the yard and shouted 'Mary Ann!' several times in various directions. But the only response was an echo from barn walls and the indignation of a bunch of scratching hens, the only visible livestock about the yard of Slickensides. Then the creamery door opened again and the three men came out. Durden elaborately locked up again, then saw the Londoners to the gate. Brunt waited until he had gone back indoors, then came out of hiding and climbed a wall into a field, thus getting himself away from Slickensides without being seen.

As he came into the rectangular space that was the nerve-centre of Walderslow, he saw two people coming down the hill from the direction of the Ashbourne road. They were Ted Milward and Mary Ann—together, but not close—perhaps a full yard between them. Brunt turned his back towards them and concentrated on their reflections in the window of the post office as they passed. Again he could see that the girl was at the point of balance of an intense personal crisis. Physically she was at the zenith of her maturity. Every eligible man—and a few others besides— in Walderslow and the villages around must in his time have lost sleep and appetite over her. But she could not hide the fact that something monstrous was amiss with her: there was no life in her gait. Ted Milward was saying something that she clearly did not want to hear. She swung bad-temperedly away from him. He left her and came over to Brunt. They watched her go round the corner towards Slickensides.

'If I were that young lady's mother, I'd be asking her personal questions before she's much older,' Milward said.

'I talked to Durden yesterday, but I could make very little of him. I know very little about the family—and even less about the Brittlebanks.'

By common accord they moved over to the wooden bench that was normally the forum of the old men of the village: it was still a little early in the raw day for them to have turned out.

'There's no denying that Septimus Durden is the life and soul of the Pig o' Lead. He's spent as much time and money in there as any other six Walderslowites put together, but he's a different man altogether when he's at home—sour-tempered, mean, fierce with his children. Since they grew up he's treated them as if they were convict labourers. And he's a bad farmer into the bargain—though he'd lay any man flat on his back if he heard him say so. He doesn't stick at anything. He could have made himself a comfortable income from his cheese, but he can't stand doing the same job over and over again. If it wasn't for Ellen Durden, Slickensides cheese would be off the market by now. God knows how many hundredweights he's lost in his time through bad pressing and slipshod storage. It's supposed to be the spores in the cave air that are the secret of it, but there's a difference between a green vein and a dusty mould right through to the centre. And I wouldn't like to say how many gallons of milk he's lost through mastitis—and ten to one that's through dirty husbandry. Oh, he's a genial soul over a pot in the Pig, but there's not a man jack in there who doesn't know him for what he is—though there's not a one of them dare say so to his face.'

Milward sat forward on the bench with his big hands clasping his splayed-out knees.

'And yet he prides himself that he's a cut above the rest of us, expects us to treat him as if he's some sort of quality. He'd like to have it thought that the Durdens are somebody, just because his great-grandfather emigrated from across the Dove: God knows what's all that special about Staffordshire. But I'll give the Durdens their due: they're not tenants. There aren't many freeholders within five miles of Walderslow—and there were no charges on Slickensides until three years ago. And that's the beginning of a rot that has the rest of its course still to run.'

Brunt asked no questions. He waited for Milward to go on.

'It had been a bad year for farmers—not Durden's fault this time. But he could have weathered it if his drinking had left him any reserves. Foot and mouth—not a herd this side of Ashbourne escaped. The milk yield practically dried up. He had hardly any of his own, but he went on making cheese with what he could buy for what he had to pay. And still he went on talking as if there was some sort of family treasure hidden down in that old lead-working. Somebody put it to him, if he'd got the mint down there that he said he had, why didn't he borrow from himself? All he did was look black—and go and see Horatio Brittlebank. That could only have been for a mortgage on Slickensides—but, mind you, nobody has any proof of that. What they transacted was never made known. The tale everybody had was that Durden had sold Brittlebank the field they call Middle

Furlong. Not that I would say personally that that was
any great loss. And it's anybody's guess what Brittlebank
thought he might make of that scraggy patch. Losing it split
Septimus's holding in two, so there had to be an easement
to give him a right of way. But you know, Tom, a man
takes pride in what he owns, especially when it's land, and
especially when his name's Durden. And if Septimus let as
much as an acre go, it could only have been because he
sniffed bankruptcy upwind. I don't think he's ever paid
young Humphrey a penny for working for him.'

'The lad doesn't seem to have much to say for himself.'

'He's not as dull-witted as you'd think from trying to talk
to him. He just isn't fond of opening his mouth—perhaps
that's because it's so long since anybody took notice of
anything he did say.'

'And the girl? I keep looking at her,' Brunt said.

'Growing up. Well—grown. She and Bill Cartledge's son
were childhood sweethearts. He's a teacher now, over at
Sterndale Cross. A steady lad—perhaps Mary Ann was
beginning to think he looked too steady to give her much
fun. But the garden probably seemed rosy enough to both
of them till young Brittlebank came home.'

'Tell me something about the Brittlebanks.'

'Money made in a foundry in Rotherham, two generations
back, when everything on the face of the earth had to be
made of cast iron. But Horatio's taken no active hand in the
business since his father died. We've yet to see whether this
is going to turn out another clogs-to-clogs story. Young
Barnard might survive: I believe he's come into a pile from
his mother's side. Horatio is tight, clever—and knows how
to be a gentleman as long as it costs him nothing. He's been
heard to boast that he treats everybody alike, and so he does
—except anybody who owes him a ha'peny—or who looks
as if he might be lacking in natural respect. It's possible to
get on all right with Horatio Brittlebank. He wants a quiet
life before anything else, and he'll pass the time of day civilly

with any man who's never offended him.'

'And his son?'

'Hasn't endeared himself to Walderslow—ever. It wasn't that he was saucy as a lad—though he was, and up to all manner of tricks. But Walderslow didn't mind that: we've all been lads ourselves. He was not beyond knocking about now and then with some of the village boys—Humphrey Durden and William Cartledge among them. But he never lost a chance to remind them where they belonged. He'd make fun of the way they spoke and the things they were ignorant about. It got worse after he went away to school. Came the long holidays, and neither side wanted much to do with each other any more.'

Milward examined his horny knuckles.

'Then he went to Oxford and didn't always come home for the holidays. He finished last year and we heard he was doing the Grand Tour. Since he came back, he's been a right bugger up and down. He's going to be here more or less permanently, it's been said, learning estate management for the day it's all his. Nobody begrudges him that—it's the natural sequence of life—but he's behaving as if he knew it all already. He's always wanting to show off what a power he's become in the land. He told Harry Lamplough at the Hall Home Farm that he'd have him evicted if he didn't do something about repairing a shed lintel. He went round personally one week, collecting cottage rents, looking round minutely at things—*for* things—to criticize: things that are no business of a landlord's, still less of a landlord's son. Like it was time Annie Heywood bought herself new curtains, those she had up let the village down. And Bert Belfield should have asked before cementing in the column of his dovecote: he'd no right to make a permanent fixture of it. Trying his wings, that's all it amounts to, but as old Bert said, if he finds they work too well, there's no telling where he might try flapping them. Then there's something he seems to have learned from someone in southern parts. He's

taken an objection to garden forks, an obsession. Says no
man can do justice to the soil with a woman's implement.
A man uses a spade, and, next time round, if Barnard
Brittlebank sees a fork in a cottager's garden, then that
family can start loading their furniture.'

'How many cottages do the Brittlebanks own?'

'I'd say two-thirds of Walderslow.'

'And is old man Brittlebank aware of what his son is
stirring up?'

'Horatio is never aware of trouble while there's some hope
that it will go away. And if it came to the push, he'd come
down as heavily as his son—smoother talk, but the same
result.'

'No feminine influence on either of them?'

'There's only one woman in their life, and she's not a
Brittlebank. Barnard's mother died within twenty-four
hours of having him. They say in the Pig that that was
because she'd seen what she'd whelped. Horatio had to find
a nurse for the child. Nurse became governess, governess
became housekeeper, housekeeper became Queen Bee.
Charlotte Machin: they say hers is the last word on most
things. She's only got to threaten to go. I don't think either
of the men has much liking for her, but she's known how to
make herself indispensable, and that's how she keeps things.
There's no serious gossip about anything between her and
the old man, though of course in the Pig they wag dirty
tongues.'

'What age of a woman is she?'

'She must have been a raw youngster when she started.
I'd put her on the forty mark.'

'And does she have much to do with the village?'

'She doesn't like us, doesn't trust us. Thinks herself several
cuts above us. She makes more on that score than the
Brittlebanks do.'

'As you'd expect. So it's either the Durdens or the
Brittlebanks who've called in Sherlock Holmes?'

'I hardly think that Septimus—'

'What about his wife? She's the one who reported the break-in—a woman who does things in her own way without consultation.'

'True. But I can't see how Ellen Durden would know how to get in touch with a man like Harlow.'

'She must see a paper or periodical once in a while, mustn't she? Harvey Harlow probably advertises his services now and then—in agony columns and so on. Don't you think so, Ted? Even the daughter might have penned him a laborious letter.'

'Not impossible. Especially if she's as desperate as she might be.'

'I'm going to see Mr Brittlebank, Ted.'

'You'll find Sherlock has got there before you. I saw him going that way as I was coming down with Mary Ann.'

'All the better,' Brunt said. 'The ground will be dug for me.'

He stood up, pointlessly shook the creases in his heavy and shapeless overcoat, stamped his feet twice and set off towards the Hall.

CHAPTER 4

At Walderslow Hall Harvey Harlow was talking impressively and Horatio Brittlebank was being impressed. He appeared on the surface to be an affable man. He knew all the outward tokens of affability and was taking pleasure in displaying them, which, if Ted Milward's diagnosis was correct, meant that he did not attach much importance to whatever Harvey Harlow had come here to say.

Walderslow Hall was three-quarters of a century old, was rudimentarily Palladian—that is, except for four false

Corinthian pillars, its façade was almost aggressively plain. It was a ridiculously large residence for a widower, his frequently absent son and their enigmatic housekeeper. Whatever other domestic staff Brittlebank kept were not in evidence: the old man was in the vast entrance hall talking to Harlow and Topliss, and himself opened the door to Brunt. He was short in stature, well tabled in girth, bald except for a greyish white area at the back of his head, moderately florid and slightly short-sighted, to correct which he wore spectacles almost as narrow and ancient as those that Brunt had exhibited in the Pig o' Lead.

The furnishings were predominantly those of the period of Queen Anne. They had been lovingly polished for a couple of centuries, and probably included many valuable pieces. But Horatio Brittlebank moved about his home as if unconscious of them, as he was of his early Wedgwood bowls and figures, and of the gallery of portraits in oils hanging in such gloomy shadows that even their closest kin might hardly have recognized them.

'Inspector, indeed? Surely that's a rank we rarely see in Walderslow? I hope to goodness you're not here to spread despondency—like these two gentlemen from London. They are trying to tell me there's something queer about Barnard going away. I don't know where they can have got such an idea from, and they absolutely refuse to tell me who's sent them up here. Somebody stony-broke that he owes a card-debt to, I shouldn't wonder, the young monkey. Or else some young baggage who's trying to get her claws into his inheritance.'

Brittlebank laughed with an ageing brand of boisterousness. The seam of potential geniality in the man was at least subcutaneous, it appeared. As far as Brittlebank was concerned, his son had got himself into a kind of scrape not uncommon among unattached males of his age, and up to now he seemed to find it extremely amusing.

'You think—?'

The old man looked over at Harvey Harlow with a different kind of amusement.

'Inspector, I'm going to ask Mr Harlow to repeat something for your benefit. If you wouldn't mind, Mr Harlow—'

Brittlebank brought something out of his waistcoat pocket and extended it towards the self-proclaimed prototype of Holmes. But Harlow did not seem very keen to cooperate. Brittlebank looked in appeal to Brunt.

'I challenged this émigré from Baker Street to show me his powers, Inspector. He asked me for a sight of some small personal possession so I handed him this.'

It was a small silver snuffbox, tarnished in places, highly polished in others from its decades of contact with the insides of pockets.

'Now, Harlow, don't be reticent in front of the Inspector. Let him see what you can do. Tell him what you have just told me.'

'Yes, let's see your flair, Harlow,' Brunt said, taking out his handkerchief to pat his eyes. Brittlebank thrust the box into Harlow's hand.

'I would have thought it was obvious—'

Harlow was still reluctant to perform again in front of Brunt. But Brittlebank left him no choice: he had to make a start.

'I told him that it was an object that had not always belonged to him, and that it had come into his possession between ten and fifteen years ago.'

'It stands out a mile that it was made before Mr Brittlebank was born,' Brunt said. 'It has been in use for longer than his lifetime. That, plus a stab or two of guess-work—'

Harlow shrugged his shoulders, modestly deprecating his talents and refusing to be discountenanced if others were reluctant to appreciate them.

'I pointed out that the previous owner was lame in his

left leg and also left-handed. Mr Brittlebank on the other hand is right-handed—and incidentally has changed his favourite brand of snuff within the last three years.'

'Truly remarkable!'

Brittlebank was overwhelmed by this cleverness. Harlow stopped talking, evidently considering himself now relieved of the danger of extending his demonstration. But Brunt was not prepared to let him escape yet.

'Well, go on, Mr Harlow—that's only the first half of your act. Tell us how you came to these egregious conclusions.'

Harlow's shoulders twitched again.

'I see nothing to be especially proud of, Mr Brunt. You yourself have already pointed out what is obvious about the age of the box. The lame left leg is apparent from the uneven wearing of the metal as it has rubbed against its previous owner's hip. As for his left-handedness, it does not surpass the wit of man to see which of his thumbnails he used to lift the lid, and over what period of time.'

He stretched out an arm and offered the box to Brunt.

'Now let's see what a professional can do.'

Brunt took the box, turned it over in his unsupple fingers and handed it back to Brittlebank without appearing to pay much attention to it. He could see that it had been in its time a valuable piece, but that to Brittlebank it was simply an object of everyday utility.

'No, Inspector?' Harlow said, with unctuous satisfaction, as Brunt seemed stumped for anything to say. Brunt was to describe the scene later for the benefit of Ted Milward.

'Of course, he thought he'd turned the tables, thought I was no end of a fool. He had been afraid I was going to expose him there and then—and then it suddenly looked as if I was the one who was going to lose face. But what does a fellow with a face like mine care about losing it? I'll be grinning all over my ugly old mug tomorrow, and with a bit of luck, the whole of next week. We'll see then what sort of a look Harvey Harlow is wearing—because, Ted, that

snuffbox did tell me something. It told me who has hired
Harvey Harlow. But that's something I'm keeping to myself
for the time being. I couldn't ask for a better advantage.'

And in that moment of gaining advantage, Brunt's attention was diverted by something else. His eyes were taking
in all they could find. He raised them to see that the four
men were not alone in the immense manorial space. On a
balustraded landing that ran laterally above the entrance
hall from the top of the pretentious master-staircase, a
woman was standing, so motionless that anyone might have
missed seeing her. She was a small woman, neatly turned
out but not attractive, and might have been an effigy in a wax
museum. There was no doubt that she had been listening to
every word that had been said. And what was the meaning
of the look on her face? What was going through her mind?
What was she expecting to happen?

Was she afraid of something? Brunt did not pitch it as
high as fear. Apprehension was perhaps nearer the mark.

He took the stage-management of the scene into his own
hands.

'There's some confidential business I'd like to discuss
with you, Mr Brittlebank—that is, unless these gentlemen
from 212c Baker Street wish to give further evidence of their
prowess.'

Harlow was tall enough to look down haughtily on Brunt.

'Indeed no, sir. I may need to call back later, in which
case I shall again beg your leave and time.'

'You'll be welcome, sir,' Brittlebank said. 'And I would
dearly love to see more of your skills, perhaps even to hear
some of your reminiscences.'

Harlow executed a stiff little bow and Brittlebank led him
to the door. As he was leaving, he raised his eyes for a
second or two towards the woman on the landing. But
without betraying the nature of his curiosity, Brunt was
unable to study her as he would have liked.

'I'm sorry to intrude even further on your time, sir,'

he said, when he and Brittlebank were alone except for
the eavesdropper. 'That man who's just left interests
me.'

'A most extraordinary fellow. I hope, Inspector, that you
have not got it in for him for childish reasons of professional
jealousy?'

There was something mischievous and teasing in
Brittlebank's tone. It seemed he was indeed a clubbable
man—in his better moods.

'Not at all. A man of remarkable wit and perception. I
take it he was right about your snuffbox?'

'Perfectly. The thing was a minor legacy from a great-
uncle—chap who half a century ago shot off his knee-cap
in the butts.'

'But why does Harlow think there's something untoward
about your son's absence?'

'As I said just now, I expect that some creditor or scheming young woman has put him on to it—it could be some
tradesman whose account he's overlooked. Very slack about
their business arrangements, the youth of today, don't you
find? It isn't that he hasn't got the money. He's worth half
as much again as I am. From his mother's side.'

'And there really was nothing abnormal about your son's
going?'

'Nothing at all. He's gone to London. He finds life intoler-
ably quiet in Walderslow. He'd been talking for some weeks
about having a change.'

'And when did he actually go?'

'Tuesday of last week. But really, Inspector, do you
consider all this necessary? Harlow asked me these same
questions—I thought the man was going to start trying to
bully me.'

'It's just that when people start talking in public about
someone being missing, my curiosity won't stand the strain.
There's always the chance that I might be set on to finding
him. I came to the village for quite a separate piece of

business. How does your son travel when he goes to London?'

'Unless he's come in his damned motor-car—which I hate to see in these grounds—thank God it's off the road much of the time—he usually takes a carriage to Buxton, where he gets on the Midland Railway to pick up the express at Miller's Dale. We saw him off—from here. Didn't we, Miss Machin?'

Brittlebank had seen his housekeeper come down the stairs, but Brunt had his back to her.

'What was that, Mr Brittlebank?'

Could she possibly have the nerve to pretend that she had not been listening? Her voice was quiet but confident, respectful of her employer, but not subservient. From the way she looked at Brunt, he judged that she did not consider police inspectors to be on a social par with the Brittlebanks —or for that matter with herself.

'Did you see Mr Barnard off in his carriage, Miss Machin?'

'Of course.'

How does a policeman know when his subject is telling a lie? A second of visible hesitation? Undue emphasis? a distaste for the untrue words as they are spoken? Miss Machin was sharp to take the initiative.

'What question arises?' she asked peevishly.

'Oh, nothing, miss,' Brunt said. 'There's been some silly talk. I no longer think it's worth pursuing.'

Which was as good a way as any of continuing to pursue it—

'I suppose he went down to Buxton in your own carriage?'

Brittlebank laughed, but not as if it was at something funny.

'As a matter of fact, he didn't. I'm afraid my son suffers a little from the superiority of his years. He looks down on everything that belongs to me. He always claimed that my carriage is about to fall to pieces, and that on this occasion he didn't fancy a wheel coming off at Gutton Bridge, so that the coachman would have to carry his portmanteaux by hand. Isn't that the sort of thing he said, Miss Machin?'

'He has a strong sense of fun,' she said, in a tone that implied that she derived her amusements from different sources.

'So how did he travel this time?'

'He hired his wheels from some jobber in one of the villages.'

'You don't know which village?'

'We have something better to do in this household than probe the trivialities of each other's lives, Mr Brunt. I do believe you're in danger of taking this nonsense seriously.'

'I am in no such danger at all. I just said that I think that nonsense is the word for it. And as I've also just said, this has nothing to do with my reason for being here. But when people are setting up rumours, I always find it convenient to have my facts marshalled in advance, where facts are available.'

The old man was too well bred to ask outright about Brunt's official business in Walderslow. Brunt was therefore compelled to make a direct approach.

'There seems to have been an attempt to break in at Slickensides Farm. Do you know anything about the Durdens, sir?'

'The man's a typical farmer of the district,' Brittlebank said. 'Produces a very fine cheese. Though I've always thought there's as much good fortune as skill behind that. Some sort of fungus in the air of the place where he stores it—that's how the story goes: the entrance-boring for what used to be a lead-mine.'

'Somebody told me that when they were boys, your son and the Durden lad used to knock about together.'

'Somebody told you that? Somebody must need something to talk about, then. Oh, it's true that once or twice

the pair of them spent an afternoon together in the hills—
before Barnard went to public school, that is. I was never
too worried about anything he got up to before he went to
school.'

Brittlebank did not suggest for a moment that he thought
that Brunt's attitude to schooling and *esprit de corps* might in
any way differ from his own. Brunt had been educated at
an elementary school in a shirtsleeve street in Chesterfield.

'I knew that once he had lived for a term among his own
kind, he'd find his own level. I never had any worries on
that score. And perhaps you've met the Durden youth?'

'Briefly.'

Brunt was almost on his way through the great front door
when Brittlebank had a worried afterthought. He screwed
up his eye-sockets so that the pupils became dark little
piercing points behind which suspicion and obstinacy were
beginning to ferment.

'Inspector—I do understand that you have your duties
to do. But somebody breaking into Septimus Durden's dairy
—that I am sure will not take up much more of your time.
Some village drunk getting an obsessive idea into his head
as he staggers home from the Pig o' Lead, I don't doubt. It
can have nothing to do with Walderslow Hall. I wouldn't
want very much more of my time held in fee answering
questions about things that neither concern nor interest me.
Goodbye, Inspector.'

Brunt walked out of Brittlebank's grounds along a dusty
white drive lined with horse-chestnut trees that autumn had
already stripped of most of their leaves. The day was dry,
the sky was a bowl of colourless, sunless uniformity. He did
not go back into the village, but took the road towards
Parsley Hay. For the second time that day he left the parish
borders of Walderslow. This time the village really did
believe that he had gone elsewhere to get on with other
work.

*

The activities of Walderslow went on, to all appearances unaffected by whatever had brought a detective-inspector and a pair of dressy amateurs on to the stage. Women beat rugs hung over their clothes-lines, turned butter-churns and donkey-stoned their doorsteps: there was a competitive domestic pride in the village that ruthlessly made and broke reputations. Men drilled holes for shot-firers at the quarry-face, forked dung and were half conscious of the hours as they chimed in the church tower. Three-quarters of a mile away to the south-west, in a field known for centuries as Cotter's Piece, a small farmer by the name of Weston was out counting the heads of his stock and making a judgement about his next marketing day. He was surprised to see that a drinking-trough, fed by a conduit from a hill-spring some fifty yards further up the dip, was down below licking level. He went up the dip and found the spring dry: a spider had stretched her web from stone to stone across a gap that would surely have been under water in any but an exceptionally dry season—and it had been a wet autumn in Walderslow. Even in high summer there was always at least a trickle from Cotter's Spring.

Frank Weston was puzzled. This gave him problems—but they were soluble. There were ways, admittedly laborious, of getting water into Cotter's Piece. He must remember to set his hired man on to it. It did not occur to him to mention this to anybody else.

Septimus and Ellen Durden both saw Mary Ann slink with rounded shoulders across the yard when she came back from walking down the village hill with Ted Milward. Septimus got up and went out into the yard himself with something of the slow-moving deliberation that had characterized his movements the day, seven years ago, when he had gone out to beat his son insensible with his buckle-belt.

Mary Ann, moving stealthily in the narrow space between a granary and a shippon, heard the opening and shutting of the house door. She heard her father's purposeful footsteps on the stone setts. His shoulder brushed against the granary wall and he entered her escape route between the outbuildings. But Mary Ann had the speed of a she-cat. Septimus stumbled over a broken old tub. By the time he had worked his way the length of the walls, his daughter was no longer in sight. He did not know whether she had gone to the right or the left or elsewhere.

In the kitchen his wife was stirring meal and water for oatcakes. The moment her husband was out of the house, she pushed the bowl away from her, and as soon as he was out of sight between the walls, she too came out. But she did not try to squeeze through any narrow gaps. She turned left, as if she were heading for Middle Furlong, but went no further than a low, dilapidated construction that had once housed crushing equipment for the mine that had preceded the farm.

Humphrey Durden was now in the creamery, staring at the cheeses as if he was expecting something spontaneous to happen to them at any moment. He was aware of these goings-on, as of a flicker of shadows across the dingy windows in front of him. He did not appear to pay heed to them, but went on waiting for some gesture from the cheeses. May Ann's mother went into the broken down crushing-shed, where the girl was standing stock still in one of the most shadowy corners. Ellen Durden seemed to know exactly where her daughter would be.

'Now, young lady, we have a few things to talk about. You must surely know one way or the other by now.'

Morning business in the Pig o' Lead was never brisk. Such of the village's males as could liberate themselves from work could only do so for a few stolen minutes, interrupting some craftily managed errand. One of those to do so today was Albert Clayton, Brittlebank's gardener, coachman and handyman, who was on his way to collect a consignment of fencing stakes at Parsley Hay. Apart from him there were only two old men, both past working age and capacity. One of them could afford the pint that would give him the freedom of the inn for as long as he kept a drop in his pot. The other had no such funds this morning, but was allowed a corner of settle within sight of the fire in consideration of fifty years of previous custom.

'They knew better than that in the old days,' Jethro Bretherton, the first man, said.

'They did that.'

'It isn't that the Old Man has it in for anybody in particular. Anybody who goes in any of those old workings with his heart in the right place has nothing to be afraid of from the Old Man.'

'But the Old Man doesn't like interference. You wouldn't get me down any of those places.'

'But they went, it was not all that many years ago, them three lads. I was on my way over to Sterndale Cross, with two ferrets and my bag-nets, so you can be certain I wasn't all that anxious to show myself. And Peter Goodwin saw them come out. It was the time he was seeing more than a Christian should of Matty Morgan's wife, and he'd gone to sweep her chimney for her, Matty being away for the afternoon walling for Wilbur Perkins. They'd been a long time underground, those three had, and one of them was hurt. Septimus's lad. He was lucky to get away with no more than he did.'

'He was lucky ever to be got out again at all. And that wasn't by the way he went in.'

'Septimus nearly killed him. And he had to wait two weeks at that, before he dared lay leather on him. There's something down there that Septimus doesn't want any man to see.'

'Something worth a fortune to him, I've heard him make out.'

'If that's the case, why didn't he go down there for a few

hundred quids' worth when he needed it? It isn't his any
more now, is it? He had to sell Middle Furlong to Brittlebank
to keep going.'

'But it's still Septimus's mine, isn't it? And he's not
working it. He's never worked it. It's not been worked since
his grandfather's day. All that Brittlebank has got to do is
nick his stowe. The laws of the old liberty still hold.'

'Young Brittlebank'll be pushing his father. That's if he
doesn't take the law into his own hands. Them of us as live
the longest will see what we shall see.'

Brittlebank's gardener drained the settled suds of his
small beer and wished them good-day.

'Now which of us said too much, do you reckon?' Jethro
Bretherton wondered. 'He'll report every word we've said,
back at the Hall, you know.'

'Are you not feeling well this morning, Miss Machin?'

There was always an archaic formality between Brittlebank and his housekeeper, even when they were alone
together.

'It's nothing,' she said unconvincingly.

But she looked as if she was feeling the cold. Charlotte
Machin did have these off periods every few weeks. Horatio
Brittlebank dreaded them. They meant that the common-
place patterns of his life were sometimes skimped. If she
was not perpetually chasing the char who came in three
days a week from the village, then the cleaning and dusting
were only half done. If she was not for ever on Cook's heels,
meals sometimes even came to the table late. Brittlebank
never expressed sympathy with Miss Machin when she was
feeling off colour. For one thing, he was not naturally
sympathetic to the discomfort of others. He would have
had to exercise his imagination to achieve that; and in
Brittlebank's eyes anything fanciful was an unmasculine
attitude. And for another thing, he did not want to say
anything that might encourage her to indulge herself. Two

days of strained routines were bad enough, without risking extending them to a third.

Brittlebank was not given to projecting himself into Miss Machin's being—or indeed into the feelings of anyone else. Otherwise he might have connected her air of preoccupied remoteness with the visits he had had this morning from men asking questions.

Those questions combined with Miss Machin's indisposition to make Brittlebank moody. He mixed himself a brandy and soda, which appeared to give him no lift whatever. He carried his glass over to the window and looked moodily out along the drive: and was in time to see Clayton returning with the cob in the shafts of a brake loaded with chestnut palings. Brittlebank was not at this distance satisfied with the grooming of the cob. Moreover, he thought he detached a looseness of the traces that was likely to lead to uneven wear. He looked upon any such fault as a public advertisement of careless management.

He would go down and admonish Clayton. Clayton's temperament lent itself ideally to the sort of relief that Brittlebank needed when he was irritated or frustrated.

Driven by Henry Drabble, who had a trap for hire in Walderslow, Harvey Harlow and Dr Topliss made a tour of several other hiring stables in the locality and ended up at Jedediah Nall's at Lowcock's End. Jedediah Nall's was neither an extensive nor an impressive equine establishment. But then, Lowcock's End was not an impressive settlement. It was unknown to many men who lived less than ten miles away. Even if you were looking for Lowcock's End, it was difficult to find, and most men who got there at all did so because they were lost on the way to somewhere else.

Nall was trusted by few men. Nall had done time for stealing by finding, for being found in an enclosed yard for an unlawful purpose, and for going equipped for stealing. If Nall ever sold a horse that fell short of what he had told

the purchaser about it, this was not only because he was
making money on the deal; it was because it would have
been unnatural for him to have sold a horse in any other
way. It was unnatural for him to tell the truth in any first
instance. To do so would have seemed to him simple-
minded, the way to throw a possible opportunity away. But
Harvey Harlow and Nall appeared to get on very well with
each other. Perhaps that was because Nall instinctively
recognized that here was a man who was big in the sub-world
in which he himself was insignificant.

A farmer called Brindley was in one of the less frequented
segments of his holding, looking over ewes immobilized on
their knees with foot-rot. He was surprised by the sogginess
of the ground. About half way up a shallow concavity that
scarcely qualified for the title of a clough, water sucked up
about the soles of his boots and at one point he sank in
almost ankle-deep.

This was normally well-drained ground, since there was
a natural outfall downhill, where a fault in the limestone let
in water as if the terrain were porous. The hills about
here were an uncharted warren of holes and channels, and
wherever water found its way to the lime, it gnawed away
the rock and sluiced about in the hollows so that in some
places there were caverns large enough to build a parish
church in. No one had ever mapped them out. In Matlock
and Castleton and Buxton there were caves open to the
public, so skilfully laid with paths and galleries that bath-
chairs and invalid carriages could be taken through them.
No one knew for certain what might lie under the fields of
Walderslow. Every generation of new young men had made
its attempts to explore, always unscientifically and often
with reckless disregard for the dangers involved, and there
were unconfirmed tales of mighty underground chambers.
What was certain was that this morning water was flowing
copiously from some part of the system out over Farmer

Brindley's fields. There seemed to be no harm it could do
in this agricultural dead-end, and Brindley, by no means
unfamiliar with minor disasters, had put it out of his mind
before he had gone much further on his round. It was not
his land to worry about, in any case. He rented it from
Brittlebank.

Brunt returned to Walderslow that evening, but did not
make any approach to anyone—not even to Ted Milward.
He went into the Pig o' Lead at about the hour when the
congregation there had stabilized itself for the session and
seated himself at a table some way away from the main
source of illumination, thereby successfully conveying the
suggestion that he did not care to participate in the delibera-
tions of the main company. Holmes and Watson, it seemed,
had opted for an early supper and had gone out to keep an
appointment, no one knew with whom.

The Pig o' Lead was not exactly oppressed by the presence
of a police inspector—but neither did men converse as
carelessly as they might have done if he had not been there.
Brunt listened to them with every appearance of being on
the brink of dozing off. No one would willingly betray
anything vital to him, and in the interests of general safety
it was considered ideal not to convey anything to him at all.
In these parts cooperation with the law was akin to going
against nature, but somebody, sooner or later, was likely to
let something slip.

The conversation was louder than it would normally have
been, an offshoot of their self-consciousness. It was mostly
anecdotal. They seemed to derive some sort of contentment,
perhaps even a communal sense of security, from repeating
the familiar. There were stories told tonight that must surely
be told in here two hundred nights in every year. Each knew
which of the others to feed, and how to get him going.
Tonight there was a preference for boisterous narrative, and
there was a constant spiralling towards the superstitious,

the supernatural: the things the two old men had talked of in here this morning. Both of them were now relatively silent.

'The Old Man will let it go so far, then he'll draw the line. Something will happen down there.'

'If you ask me, something's happened down there already.'

Always the pivot was this mythological Old Man. Like *Slickensides*, the *Old Man* was a blunderbuss term, with overlapping connotations. The *Old Man* was the debris of everything that had gone on since man had first scarred these hills: the spoil-heaps were called the *Old Man*, and so were the tool-marks in the rock-face, the horizontal wooden climbing stemples, rotting across the width of vertical shafts. The *Old Man* was the name given to every trace of the ancient miner: he went back to Roman and Saxon times. But he was also a ghost—the amalgamated ghost of every old miner who had ever torn at the rock. He could be heard about his patrols by anyone who entered one of his old workings in a sufficiently sensitive frame of mind. Those who believed implicitly in the Old Man were not particularly afraid of him. He was not in general malevolent, was even known in his oblique way to have given a helping hand to those who came back into his domain in like mind to himself. It was believed that the Old Man would help a new miner to find a seam, or warn him away from an impending roof-fall—only there were no new miners these days. Some years ago Laurie Wilde's old collie fell into a crumbling shaft over on Pennyfold Rake. But the creature survived because he found the carcase of a sheep trapped in like fashion, and lived on that. Laurie Wilde and Benjamin Stone went down on a rope to get the dog out, and when they had freed him, they heard the Old Man, walking away into the inner silence of his galleries. The Old Man liked to keep his eye on things.

But there was also a belief, not substantiated by anything

that anyone could point to, that there was a limit to what the Old Man would put up with in the way of disturbance. Disrespect, wanton destruction in the wake of his industry —these were things that he would not endure beyond a certain point; and the company in the Pig o' Lead saw no reason why he should.

'If you ask me, something's happened down there.'

'I can tell you straight—it has.'

They all turned to look at a man who had had nothing to say so far: Jud Wetherall, Frank Weston's hired man.

'I had to traipse back and forth up Cotter's Piece with twenty yoke of buckets this morning. The spring's stopped.'

'Funny—'

Jack Will Harmer, a strange man with a nose that had been flattened in a boyhood fight—

'I took a short cut over Walter Brindley's middle field— and it was sodden. I've never known that happen there before. Something must have shifted under there.'

Brunt blinked sleepily.

CHAPTER 5

Charlotte Machin knew exactly where she belonged. But it took Brunt some time to understand that and other things about her.

He understood well enough that it was within the internal boundaries of any particular social class that subtle distinctions were most jealously preserved. The working class had its own upper, middle and lower categories, who scorned the strata beneath them. Miss Machin had no doubt that it was within the upper segment that her tap-roots had been nourished. Her father had been a master coppersmith with his own contracting workshop that had his name over the door. They had been a large, though not a needy family, but their father had seen no virtue in allowing his grown-up daughters unearned leisure. He had manœuvred Charlotte into a post as uncertificated teacher. But this had not worked. There had been a primitive independence about the street-reared boys of Standard Four whom she had been set to manage: a crude spirit of assertion from which she had been sheltered throughout her formative years. She could not teach them—could not even succeed in keeping them in their desks. Deserting that school without regard for the terms of her contract was one of the few displays of initiative that she ever made in her young life. It came in fact as a relief to her headmaster, who was thereby saved from the embarrassing procedures of getting rid of her.

She next went into a private household as governess, and took so naturally to her nicely bred new charges that after a couple of years there she was able to present an impeccable testimonial when Horatio Brittlebank advertised for help in his tragedy. For her first few years with him she listened patiently for hours while he extolled the beauties and virtues of his lamented wife. He was a desperately lonely man who could not understand what had happened to his life. After absurd months of eating separately, in rooms far distant from each other in the great house, she suggested joining him at his table—her second show of initiative, and an extremely forward one in those days. But if she harboured any romantic feelings towards her employer, she suffered them in martyred silence until they were neutralized by the passing of the years: Horatio Brittlebank was a man of obstinate sentimental loyalty but blunted feelings, and had no intention of ever falling in love and marrying again. Very rarely was he critical of anything she did or said, but he could sulk frighteningly for days at a time when he was displeased by something that he was keeping to himself. Gradually she learned most but not all of the things that could bring this about and steered mostly clear of them, even though that meant pandering pathetically to his whims. By the time he was forty, he was a spoiled old man.

As for the baby, she trained him to use his pot, and later to stand at the pedestal. She fought to correct his moods, his tantrums and his infantile transgressions and by and large she managed them. She loved the child extravagantly, because he and nobody else was hers to love. The formation of his character became her life's purpose. She over-protected him, and when he grew old enough to roam about the hills, she worried herself to distraction over the perils that beset him. It was only when he went away to school that she saw the first chilling signs that he might grow away from her. And by then she regarded herself as a Brittlebank. Without conscious scheming, she had made herself indis-pensable to Horatio. She knew what indulgences he could not do without and indulged him accordingly. He could not live without her in his house. She accompanied him and Barnard on their outings and holidays: Horatio never out-grew a sentimental attachment to Bognor. One year they went by way of change to Bath, and once even to Boulogne: that was the highlight of her life.

Thus Charlotte Machin made the transition upwards from the class of her fathers. The Brittlebanks' tastes and judgements became hers. She read all the novels left behind by Barnard's mother—complacent tales of unthreatened gentility and an unquestioned moral code. She acquired the Brittlebanks' attitudes to food, wine, music (such as there was of it in their lives) and, when they were away from Derbyshire, the theatre. She shared their judgement of people. Her attitude to working men and their families—including masters of their trades with signboards of their own—became complex but inflexible. It was not that she was disloyal to her past. It was not that she became con-temptuous of men who worked with their hands: neither, for that matter, was Horatio Brittlebank. He had every respect, he said, for honest artisans—as long as they were honest with him. But he was acutely aware of their limitations and Charlotte, laughing in genteel fashion at his occasional near-epigrams, agreed with him without qualification—or thought. The truth about Miss Machin's feelings towards the sort of people from whose control she had escaped, was that she had become afraid of them. She did not remember the names of those Standard Four boys, but she never forgot their contempt for her.

She was also afraid of Harvey Harlow and Dr Thomas Topliss, especially on their second visit to Walderslow Hall after taking their early supper at the Pig o' Lead. She knew a little about Sherlock Holmes from two copies of the *Strand* Magazine that the adolescent Barnard had brought home, and that his father had read with zest. With the mists swirling in at the windows of London cabs, with people's ingenious methods of doing others to death, she found the first story terrifying and would certainly never read the other. And when she saw these two impostors on the premises, she was so confused that she could not properly differentiate between them and the originals.

On this second, as on their first visit, she kept them under observation from a discreet if not actually concealed vantage-point. But if they knew that she was watching them, they shrewdly kept that knowledge to themselves. She could see that whatever news they had to bring was grave. Horatio Brittlebank came down to speak to them in the hall and they played no tricks, made no flashy deductions this time. She could not catch their words, but the old man was clearly perturbed after the first few syllables. He led them at once to his study, a most unusual lowering of the barriers of privacy. He hated any kind of entertaining in the evening, hated anything to disturb his solitary digestive hour after dinner. And it went equally against the grain with him for any stranger to catch a glimpse of the unguarded secrets of his lair; not that they amounted to anything: open books about whatever enthusiasm had lately caught his fancy, framed photographs that he preferred not to be asked to identify. If he had to receive visitors, he liked to talk to them in his garden or the hall. But tonight he did not hesitate to lead these gentlemen to the study.

He was not with them as long as she expected him to be —it was hardly more than a quarter of an hour before he brought them out to the door. (He employed hardly any servants, but this was not entirely a matter of economy. He never cared to embarrass himself with any personal relationship that could be avoided.)

The detectives—if that is what they were—were not talking now and Horatio Brittlebank's features were stony. She expected him to join her in the drawing-room when they had gone: he invariably put in an appearance after his hour's retreat, but tonight he stayed away. Ten o'clock struck and even at that signal he did not emerge. She sat at her work-basket with the drawing-room door open— another departure from custom—and waited five more minutes before taking the risk of interrupting him. As a rule, if something was upsetting him, it was not usually long before he came and talked to her about it, seldom looking her in the face while he did so. It was only his increasingly rare financial transactions that he kept to himself. If he was ever silent about other worries, she always felt a foreboding —not far removed from an oblique jealousy.

Now he did not even respond to her first gentle knock on his door. She knocked harder, and was not sure whether she heard him speak or not. She gathered her courage and turned the doorknob. Horatio Brittlebank was sitting at his desk with no book open, no papers laid out. His face was a mustering thundercloud, and the capillary veins over his cheekbones, drained of their fire, were a dirty sluggish purple. There was no doubt that he resented her intrusion.

'Did you want something, Miss Machin?'

'You haven't had your drink, Mr Brittlebank.'

She always sent him to bed with a glass of whisky and

warm milk. It was unthinkable that he could ever prepare it for himself. She could not remember when he had last entered the kitchen, and she doubted whether he had ever held a pan in his hand in his life.

'Thank you. I shall not be going to bed for some time yet.'

That was a snub. He closed his lips tightly and thrust out his jaw, a peremptory order to her to mind her own business. She left the study, leaving the door staring open: an audacious counter-gesture. Brittlebank called her back.

'Miss Machin—I will not have that kind of rudeness in my house.'

She all but weakened and said she was sorry. Instead, she made a movement of her own chin, rather ridiculously an imitation of his.

'Miss Machin—you have a good deal to answer for.'

The words pierced her like arrows of ice. She knew what she most feared from these men from London. But she could not think how they could possibly be involved in it.

'What am I supposed to have done?'

Her voice did not sound to her like her own.

'If I tried to tell you, you would not understand.'

'In that case, I shall never know, shall I?'

'It is precisely because of your abysmal lack of understanding over a long period of years that things have come to the pass that they have.'

If she had been a sharper psychologist, she would have known that it was his deep personal helplessness that made him lash out at the nearest—indeed the only—available sacrificial victim. She had not known until that moment how much she hated the Brittlebanks.

'I think if you have anything to complain of, Mr Brittlebank, we had better leave it till the morning.'

'Good night, Miss Machin.'

He sounded as if he had hated her for years, too.

*

The Pig o' Lead was notionally closed, the prophets and seers having departed for their dour and grey little homes, from whose windows the lights had already been extinguished. Only Brunt remained. He had advanced from the remote seat in which he had spent the evening and was drinking a good night hot toddy with the landlord at the counter.

'You've not sorted it out yet then, Mr Brunt?'

Brunt looked at him with a touch of irony behind his watery pale eyes.

'It's sorting out what there is to sort out that's the trouble,' he said. 'If you see what I mean?'

'A lot of fuss about nothing you mean?'

'Let's hope that's how it turns out. What are they saying in here, Joe?'

'Oh, we have the brains of the Peak in here, Mr Brunt. They may not know what anything's about, but it's surprising sometimes what they think they know.'

'What are they saying when I'm not in here?'

Joe Bramwell looked a trifle uncomfortable.

'They're surprised that you're still here,' he said.

'Don't water it down to save my feelings, Joe. Aren't they saying I must be getting past it, losing my touch, taking as long as this over a broken window in a country creamery? Putting it down to old age, are they?'

'Nay, Mr Brunt. They think better of you than that.'

'Maybe I shall get more than one fish on the same line,' Brunt said, knowing that that would track round the Pig's clientele before tomorrow was old.

Then there were the sounds of someone unaccustomed to its temperament struggling with the outside latch. The landlord went over to let in Harvey Harlow and his companion and to shoot the king bolts behind them. Harlow caught sight of Brunt's glass and ordered the same for himself and the doctor.

'Had a good day, Inspector?'

'Passable. I hope you can say at least the same, Mr Harlow.'

'Oh yes. We have completed what we came here to do. We intend to be back in the metropolis tomorrow night.'

'I'm glad to hear it,' Brunt said, in a tone too sweet for Harlow openly to suspect him of sarcasm. 'And may I ask how Horatio Brittlebank reacted to the news you just took him?'

Harlow looked theatrically surprised.

'You saw which way we went, I presume?'

'On the contrary, Joe will confirm that I have not moved from here all the evening. Perhaps you'd care for an explanation of *my* plodding virtuosity?'

'I would be delighted. We are, after all, comrades in arms.'

There was a suave courtesy about Harlow's style that evidently did not regard Brunt as a serious competitor in any situation.

'It was deliciously simple, really,' Brunt said. 'You called this morning at any number of stabling establishments, ending up at Jedediah Nall's. Can I therefore assume that it was Jedediah Nall who drove Barnard Brittlebank the day he left? I have no doubt you got a sworn statement about the young man's true destination. I say a sworn statement because Jeddy Nall rarely states anything without swearing.'

'I'd no idea you were such a wit, Inspector.'

'We tailor our words to the intellect of our listeners, Mr Harlow. And may I ask what *was* Barnard Brittlebank's true destination?'

'I see no harm in telling you, Inspector. The entire village is likely to know before long. Mr Barnard Brittlebank let it fall in the hearing of Mr Jedediah Nall that from Buxton station he proposed to travel to Manchester and thence to Liverpool, where he had booked a passage to Canada. He believes, it seems, that there are fortunes to be made and excitement to be had in the management of the timber forests there. And even if he does not strike lucky, he believes that he will come home with richly broadened experience. It would seem that young Mr Brittlebank has begun to find the life he has been leading since leaving the university humdrum and unrewarding.'

'I see. And how did Mr Brittlebank senior receive this intelligence?'

'I'm afraid that it hit him rather hard, Mr Brunt. Mr Barnard had not seen fit to discuss his intentions with his father before leaving home.'

'And Miss Machin? What did she feel about it?'

'It would have been inappropriate for me to have broached the matter to her. Mr Brittlebank did not pass on the news to her while we were in the house,' Harlow said. 'I do not know whether he is accustomed to discuss his son's private affairs with his housekeeper.'

'You don't?' Brunt said, with naïvely exaggerated surprise.

'How could I be expected to?'

'I would have thought that a gentleman of your perspecuity could have risen to a logical process as uncomplicated as that. Though I must confess that in the last five minutes I have changed my mind about one major issue. I was convinced until now that it was Miss Machin who has been employing you.'

'Very far from the mark,' Harlow said, with a distinct smirk of superiority.

'That I now know. I had reached that conclusion because you could only have known what you did about the snuffbox by collusion with somebody close to Brittlebank. But why should it have been Miss Machin? Is it not more logical to conclude that it was Barnard Brittlebank himself and that the main purpose of your mission is to spread this story of a purely fictitious Canadian journey?'

'That is an outrageous slander, Inspector.'

Harlow was not far from losing his temper, and Topliss's nervous discomfort was almost laughable.

'I'll not try to be clever and pass this off as entirely the result of elementary reasoning. Knowing that you had called on Jedediah, I also went to see him late this afternoon. We know each other well. I can usually dislodge truths from him, for the simple reason that I know so many other truths about him that he would prefer me to put out of my mind. And he knows that he's stuck with me in this neighbourhood for some years to come. You are a clever man, Mr Harlow. Your play with Brittlebank's snuffbox this morning was little short of brilliant. I am sure that if that piece of bric-à-brac had not been forthcoming, his son had briefed you about a range of similar objects. And I do not believe that Jeddy Nall told you anything. I believe you told him what to say. That to my mind is a field of activity closely akin to confidence trickery.'

This was totally untrue. Brunt had been nowhere near Jedediah Nall, but Harlow accepted the story as naïvely as a schoolboy. He was now exercising rigorous control over himself.

'I think you had better mind what you are saying, Inspector—in front of a witness.'

'Which witness? Joe Bramwell?'

Brunt laughed. The landlord looked up from a wooden crate that he was filling with empty bottles.

'Sorry, gentlemen—I haven't been listening—'

'You see, Mr Harlow—I am not beyond a disingenuous move or two myself. Or to put it in terms that you might be more familiar with—I'm not beyond cheating.'

Harlow took offence at that, asked for a candle and went dramatically up the stairs, Topliss following with appropriately outraged dignity.

Brunt winked at Joe Bramwell and said he must be getting back to Ted Milward's. It would not do to keep the ex-policeman out of his bed. But when he left the inn, that was not where Brunt went. He made a circuitous way through the village, leaving Slickensides behind him, but coming back to the farm territory at a point where the wall of Middle Furlong skirted a gated road to Hartington. His eyes were now adjusted to the starlight and he had no difficulty in finding an easily climbable stretch of wall. He slithered down the slope where he had seen Mary Ann sitting, followed a sheep-track down to the waterswallow and made his way up towards the farm, stubbing a toe occasionally against a loose-lying stone. When he came to the nuclear cluster of farm buildings, he took the undercover route behind the sties and the granary, looking back at the farmhouse more than once as he approached the creamery.

He had a small selection of elementary lock-picking instruments in his pocket, and without showing any light he had the door quietly open in not much more time than it would have taken Septimus Durden with his keys. One more look in the direction of the house, which was as lifeless as a grey mausoleum, and he was inside the door, which he pulled noiselessly closed behind him.

He paid no attention to the window through which the break-in had been effected, having exhausted the detective potential of that during his daytime visit. It was a smash-and-enter job that had required no skill, and had been carried out with no suggestion of care. Various bits and pieces that had stood on the sill: an oil-bottle, a packet of soap-flakes, the head of a broken hammer, a lidless tin of dried-out wax polish—had been scattered to the floor, from which no one had bothered to tidy them up.

Brunt brought out of his pocket a small electric flash-lamp, of the kind that had been a novelty when Barnard Brittlebank had owned one as a boy. Shielding it as well as he could with his hand, he moved over to a corner where a cradle for carrying cheeses was leaning against the wall. It was a part of the creamery at which he had not looked closely when he was here yesterday, because Septimus Durden had been with him and watching.

There were two wooden stanchions nailed against the wall. At first sight they looked like rudimentary buttresses, though the building had no obvious need for such support. In fact the two pieces of robust timber were the last remains of a *stowe*—the old miner's word for the scaffolding for the winding gear that had stood at the head of the shaft when this had been an active mine. A *coe* —a protective shed—had stood here, and this dairy had later been built round it. Stout flooring had been laid over the mouth of the shaft, and it was on this that the cheese cradle was standing.

Brunt bent to see whether the dust and grit on this area of floor had been disturbed here more than elsewhere in the dairy. He examined the woodwork with his light only an inch above it. Across the corner of one of the planks were close parallel marks that could have been made by stiff broom bristles. The area on his right hand, used for pressing and storing the cheeses, was clean by comparison, evidently swept now and then, though rather less frequently scrubbed. Perhaps this work was the province of young Humphrey: it was plain to see that it was being done with less than devotion. Brunt unbent and looked up above himself. What interested him now were the two struts that had once formed the overhead arms of the stowe. He ran the disc of his torchlight up and down them, stopped to examine two little notches less than an inch deep that had been cut in each of them—cleanly cut, and not all that long ago—for when he ran the tip of his finger into them, it came away with a few specks of wood dust. Then light streaked in at a weird angle through the broken window behind him, and he knew that he was trapped. Someone was crossing the yard outside with a lantern, throwing up grotesquely moving shadows of the miscellaneous creamery equipment. The door was snatched open, the lantern was shone full into Brunt's face, giving a macabre impression of pallor amid the pimples and wens.

'Here! What the hell!'

It was Septimus Durden, very angry, perhaps awakened from his sleep still more than a little drunk, and not incapable of doing violence to an intruder on the spur of the moment—even to a police inspector.

'I've found something here that'll interest you, Septimus.'

'You've no bloody right—'

'But I'm here, aren't I? That makes a pig's dinner of right and wrong, doesn't it? Stop talking about things you're not going to do anything about, Septimus. Come over here and look at this. It'll show you why somebody bothered to break into this bloody hole.'

'Do you think there's anything in here that I haven't seen thirty thousand times before?'

He came over, nevertheless, although pretending reluctance.

'No need to look further than this,' Brunt said, and pointed up at the two fresh cuts in the woodwork.

'Somebody's nicking your stowe, Septimus.'

Durden looked at the cuts closely and, as Brunt had done, tested them with his fingertip for new sawdust.

According to usages that could still be evoked before the Barmote Court, which still met formally in these former mining communities, a man who did not work his mine, or who left its entrance in a dangerous condition, could have it claimed by any other prospector who went through the appropriate forms and rituals. One of these was to warn his rival of his intentions, and he did this by *nicking his stowe*— on three separate occasions—by cutting notches in the woodwork at the head of the shaft.

'Now I wonder who could have done that?' Brunt asked.

'God knows.'

'Who'd want Slickensides Mine? Is there a workable seam left down there?'

'There might be, in some men's estimation.'

'Whose, for example?'

'How the hell should I know?'

'You've always talked as if you had the treasure of El Dorado down there, Septimus. Maybe you've been blathering in the wrong company.'

'Nay, Mr Brunt. There's nobody in Walderslow would dare to nick my stowe.'

'Nobody, Septimus? Why does it have to be somebody from Walderslow, anyway? There are rogues in other places.'

Brunt stamped on the flooring that covered the shaft, testing it for hollowness. It seemed no less solid here than was the rest of the timber.

'When was that last opened up, Septimus?'

'Regularly. We mature our cheeses down there.'

'So you're often down in the mine?'

'Only at the top. I haven't been down the adit for more than seven years. That was when that fool of a lad of mine took a fall at the bottom of the waterswallow. I had to bring him this way out.'

'You mean there's direct communication between where we are now and the waterswallow?'

'When the Old Man was working his seam, he broke through into a natural system.'

'An extensive one, I'll be bound—'

Durden looked at Brunt with a peculiar intensity.

'It was once. The seam itself is flooded deep. They struck too much water. That's why the Old Man abandoned it. You'd need a beam-engine to pump it out.'

'But you can always get from here to the waterswallow?'

'That depends on the season.'

'And what about this season?'

'You'd get through.'

'Suppose I were to tell you that there's a spring dried up in Cotter's Piece? Would you know where it normally flows out of the mine?'

'I might. But I'd say that tale's unlikely after the autumn we've had. Nothing's dried up this year.'

'Brindley's land certainly hasn't. He's got trouble the other way—he's waterlogged.'

'Brindley waterlogged? Since when?'

'He first noticed it yesterday.'

'I didn't go out yesterday, so I didn't hear anything.'

'Septimus—what could be clogging up an outlet with a head of water that's risen so high it's found another way out —from Cotter's Piece to Brindley's?'

'It could be a rock fall. It's slickensides down there. Anything could happen. When it does go off, it goes off with a bang.'

'And suppose it isn't a rock fall? What other kinds of obstruction could divert a spring?'

'I couldn't say without looking. Things can change down there. There's a lot of rock from the old borings stored up on baulks of rotting timber in the roof: old boarding, laid across the old stemples. The whole lot could come down. If a boulder cracks slickensides, it can go off like a cannon.'

'We shall have to go down there, Septimus.'

'Aye, well—thee and me together, happen, in the morning.'

Brunt could see the cunning working behind Durden's eyes. He would be down the mine alone the moment he was left here, in all likelihood destroying evidence. Even if it wasn't evidence pertinent to this case, men like Durden always had a few things they did not want authority to know about.

'*Now*, Septimus.'

'Now?'

'We don't want to draw people's attention to what we're doing, do we, Septimus?'

It was the one argument that calculated to appeal at once to Durden.

'I'll go and get ropes and tackle.'

'And get Humphrey up,' Brunt told him. 'I'll feel safer with three pairs of hands.'

CHAPTER 6

Ellen Durden did not let her husband know that she was awake. She dared not say anything, because she knew that this time, once she started to speak her mind, it would be fatal, final. She knew he had heard a footstep in the yard. She had heard it herself—had wakened sharply, for no reason, after half an hour of her first sleep and had not succeeded in escaping again from the vortex of her sicklily spinning brain.

Septimus pulled on clothes, laced his boots, breathing laboriously as he bent to them. She lay stiffly still, finding a perverse comfort in immobility. She heard him go downstairs as quietly as he could and leave the house, saw the rays from his shifting lantern as he crossed to the creamery. Only then did she stir, went to the window, saw Brunt's silhouette beyond the broken pane. It was she who had called in Brunt, and not only because of the poisoning of the dog. She knew who it was who had poisoned the dog. She knew who had broken into the dairy. Those were things that had to be brought to book by Brunt—after he had been allowed to find the answer for himself: she was not going to tell him. Once Brunt was on the scene there would be no stopping the torrent of events that would follow. There were moments when she told herself it had been madness to call him in. Brunt would slog on until he had finished, and that would not be until he saw nothing left to uproot. She knew it was on the cards that when Brunt left Slickensides later tonight, he would be taking Septimus Durden with him. There had been times in her life when she had prayed that something or somebody would take Septimus Durden from her. But now that it was likely to happen before another dawn, she did not know how she would be able to face up to all it meant. It would be the end of everything that she had ever known. Her married life had been a battle, a history of daily, hourly skirmishes, but she had accustomed herself to all that.

And what had Brunt discovered, to bring him alone to the creamery at this time of night?

She needed activity. She needed to brew a pot of tea. Septimus would want one too, when he came in again—*if* Brunt let him come in again.

She got up, pulled an outside coat over her nightgown— the Durdens did not rise to dressing-gowns—went out on to the landing as Mary Ann was coming out of her room too. She was snivelling, of course, had done nothing but whine and snivel since she had fallen in and out with Barnard Brittlebank. It was only to be expected, wasn't it? But Ellen Durden did not propose to let any sympathy with her daughter to show through. It was hard work and cold water that Mary Ann needed.

'What's happening, Mother? Why's Dad gone out?'

'He's in the creamery. With Inspector Brunt.'

They went down together to the kitchen. Mary Ann filled the kettle while her mother scraped at the wick of the two-burner oil-stove that they used when the fire was out. They might be at odds with each other, but there was no need for mother and daughter to talk over any household job that they were doing together.

But Ellen told Mary Ann to stop her snivelling.

'Pull yourself together. Life's got to go on.'

'It's all your fault.'

'My fault? It was you who thought you knew what you wanted. I knew all along that nothing would come of it, but you can't say I tried to stand in your way.'

'You shouldn't have made me write that stupid letter— it was nothing but lies.'

'You didn't know when you wrote it that it wasn't true. And it could have been true, as you know only too well.'

'Well, thank God it wasn't.'

'I told you it was the quickest way of finding out which way the wind was blowing. And you know that now for certain. He's gone.'

'As if you care.'

'I only want what's best for you. We had to find out. We've found out, and there's an end of it.'

'You have no feelings, Mother.'

'You know nothing about my feelings. I know a lot of things that you've still to learn. At your age, you still think that marriage is two people. It isn't. It's a lot of other things besides. I thought I was marrying Septimus Durden—but I married Slickensides. The sooner you go back to your schoolteacher, the better.'

'Mother, how can I? He *knows*. I don't want to, anyway.'

Did it not occur to Ellen Durden that her brand of harsh sense stood no hope of penetrating?

'He might not even have had the letter,' Mary Ann said. 'He went so suddenly.'

'Mary Ann, stop trying to kid yourself.'

'Wouldn't you disappear suddenly if somebody like my father was swearing he'd kill you?'

'Don't talk like that, Mary Ann. Don't you ever tell a soul he said that. You know how much notice to take of your father's tongue.'

The lantern came swinging unsteadily back across the yard. Septimus opened the door bluffly.

'What's going on?' his wife asked him.

'I've got to get Humphrey up. Brunt's dead set on going down the mine.'

'At this hour? What in hell's name for?'

'God knows. But the sooner he's been and seen there's nothing there, the sooner he'll be satisfied.'

Sleep was elusive in other corners of Walderslow too. In the long reaches of the night Charlotte Machin still tried—tried with her candle snuffed, then lit it again—tried to read, but had no interest in smug characters and monochrome plates, came to the end of two pages and did not know what had happened in them, or how it was connected with what had gone before.

For Charlotte Machin all was over. It wasn't last night, she knew, not yesterday that all was finished for her. Everything had been over for days now, running into weeks. She had simply not faced up to it, had lived in unfounded hope, ought to have known that it could have no foundation.

She played a mental game that she had not retreated into since she was a girl, her running-away-from-home game. She had never been a wayward child, nor had her parents been as restrictive as many in that era. But there had been times when they had fallen out with her over how life should be conducted. There had been tearful scenes, hurtful reproaches about ingratitude. Then she had fantasized about leaving home, had pictured herself in flickering images culled from a child's adventure story, crossing moors and parkland, tiptoeing through birthday-card villages before anyone was awake, sleeping in barns and dingles until they finally caught up with her and brought her home amid tears and rejoicing, all forgiven, all forgotten, a new way of life implicitly assured for one and all.

She knew that she would never have done anything of the kind. It had never been more than an inner-tearful flush of imagination. She had never had anything serious to be sorry for herself about: never until now—and now there was nowhere to fly to. Here and now at Walderslow Hall there was no hope of reconciliation, no ultimate reunion—no one to be unified with. Tomorrow—no, it was today already—she had to be away: not padding stealthily through idealized sleeping villages, not stepping over springy peat between heather-banks, like some unjustly treated angel in a Victorian romance. She would go by train, change at some windy junction for a genteel-obscure seaside resort, somewhere she had never been before, where no one she knew was ever likely to come: some town a quarter the size of Bognor, and on a northern coast, because the Brittlebanks had always had a contempt for northern coasts. She would live like a rentier on her savings and take winter walks in weak sunshine on deserted clifftops. Until everything stopped. She did not qualify her dreams with frustrating calculations as to how many seasons—how many months, for that matter —her savings were likely to last out. Or what was likely to happen then.

She would simply tell Horatio Brittlebank at breakfast-time that she was going—

Breakfast was the only meal that they did not eat together—

Breakfast was the only meal that Charlotte Machin actually cooked for Horatio Brittlebank. (Mean as he was about servants, he kept a cook, but she was someone from the village who came in later in the day. Charlotte Machin did all the dealings with Cook on his behalf. He was insufficiently domesticated to deal directly with a cook.)

Would stiff-lipped Charlotte Machin serve Horatio Brittlebank his breakfast in the morning? Or would she leave him to fend for himself, as he was going to have to fend for himself for ever after? Somehow there seemed something harsh and raw about not serving him that last meal, even if they did not speak to each other as she put it on the table in front of him.

And what if he tried to make things up while she was serving him?

She would have to let that pass over her head. Charlotte Machin had bigger troubles than had to do with Horatio Brittlebank.

Horatio Brittlebank could not sleep, either. All the acceptable rhythms of his life were on the verge of collapse.

It would not have been true to suggest that father and son

had led an agreeable existence together during Barnard's periods at home. Neither generation made any effort to understand the other's outlook. Neither attempted any curious excursion into the other's mind-world. They did not indulge very frequently in wordy battles—but neither did they ever come even to an informal agreement to differ. The old man was saddened rather than embittered that Barnard had not developed into a consoling mirror-image of himself. He hated his son for his motor-car, for the trouble he was always getting into with the police over it. He hated him for the things—and people—he had wasted his money on in Oxford. He hated him for his taste in London entertainments. He strongly suspected his attitude to women. And he blamed Charlotte Machin for everything. Whenever he suspected anything less than perfect in the character of Barnard, he always held it against Miss Machin. Indeed, there had been a time, at the period when Barnard was learning to read and write, when he had been tempted to get rid of her and make a fresh start: all those petty womanish ideas, all that working-class puritanism; all that mother-hen cackling. He had had to tell her time and again to let him behave like a boy. He had had to tell her that he was too big now for her to have to go and see if he had drowned in his bath. He had to tell her not to fuss when Barnard climbed trees and broke his knees. But Horatio Brittlebank had held on to Miss Machin, partly because a fresh start was something he could not face, and partly because he was confident that the wholesome regime of a boys' school would set things right. By and large he had believed that that confidence was not misplaced—until Barnard began coming home on vacation from Oxford. It began to be a relief when, now and then, he got himself invited to other places in his idle time.

But what now? He could bear Miss Machin no longer. He could not stand her pathetic efforts to communicate with him. Now that she no longer had Barnard to fuss over,

she was fussing over him, ludicrously convinced that she
understood the workings of his mind. No wonder the boy
had run away to Canada. And there was going to be whispering about that in the village and among his handful of
acquaintances. There were relatives that he could not avoid
seeing every two or three years—a cousin in the Royal
Navy, another in a discount house in Manchester—they
would want an explanation. Why Canada? What had got
into the boy's brain to make him want to go to Canada, just
at the time when he was beginning to be really needed at
home and about the estate? Horatio Brittlebank loathed the
idea of having to make explanations to others—even of
having to face their silent speculation. He hated people who
thought they could read his mind. He was beginning to hate
life itself.

The landlord of the Pig was famously the most inquisitive
man in Walderslow, but few puzzles had ever given his
ingenuity greater exercise than the two men who had
come under his roof with the Baker Street cachet. He
lost no opportunity for listening at their door. But nothing he had heard so far had told him anything certain
about their purpose in Walderslow. Tonight, despite the
lateness of his closing hour, he was prepared to lose even
more sleep when he heard their voices behind the woodwork.

They were falling out: not by any means the first time
that they had done so since their arrival. Topliss was the
querulous one—apparently dissatisfied about their reasons
for being here, repetitive and shrewish in the tone of his
complaints. Harlow was clearly listening to him with dimin-
ishing patience—then he shut him up, with vitriolic sarcasm.

Joe Bramwell had known within seconds of their arrival
that Topliss was not a doctor. Indeed, in order to keep up
the pretence he must surely be under orders to open his

mouth in public only in case of absolute necessity—-and that was how Topliss did appear to comport himself.

For what purpose Harlow took Topliss around with him was unimaginable. The man had no brains and such of his conversation as the public was allowed to hear was no more than routine back-up for Harlow's detective act. Topliss was like a stage artist's feed, making sure that the act got an airing, and he did not even do this well. Joe, mercifully for the peace of his house, had so far not had occasion to see Topliss called into the sort of action at which Topliss excelled, and for which Harlow employed him.

Joe could not make head or tail of the tag-ends of speech that he could hear from outside their bedroom. Whatever it was that they were doing, they were going at it with a diligence that suggested that they would be continuing until the small hours. He heard at intervals a whirring sound, as of a wheel spinning on a pivot, punctuated by a series of dry, irregular clicks and the calling aloud of numbers and colours. Joe would have thought that they were playing some game, except that there was too much quarrelling between them to suggest that they were doing something for pleasure. It seemed that everything that Topliss did displeased Harlow—as if he was exasperatingly slow at learning anything—as if he was too slow-witted to understand simple instructions that Harlow had spelled out for him over and over again. Then their bickering took on a new turn. Topliss became so angry that he raised his voice and Bramwell had no difficulty in picking up every syllable.

'We ought not to have hung on here. We ought to have cleared off straight away. I don't like that bloody policeman. I don't know what's going on behind that warthog's face of his—but he knows more than he's saying.'

'Keep your voice down, man. He knows no more than you're likely to tell him. What *can* he know?'

'I don't trust him. I don't trust that bloody coachman we

went to see. And I'm wondering how much longer I can go on trusting you. I want to get back to London.'

'Haven't I said—first train in the morning?'

'You've changed your mind before now.'

'Well, I'm not changing it this time. Do you think I'm getting any pleasure out of being in a hole like this? Listen!'

Bramwell did not know what it was that Harlow thought he had heard. No suspicious sound had penetrated out here to the landing, so it must have been something from under their window, at the other side of the house. He heard Harlow get up. Fearing that he might suddenly snatch open the door, the landlord blew out his candle and made himself scarce along the darkened corridor. He did not need a candle anywhere in this house.

Septimus Durden stooped with a bolster chisel, an iron implement for lifting floorboards, grunted over the posture that he had to adopt and brought up one of the planks that covered the entrance to the mine. Then he pushed the tool into his son's hand.

'I don't know what the hell I'm thinking about. What's the use of having a labourer and doing it yourself? Get that lot up—and stack them so we can put them back in their proper order.'

His lantern showed the blackness of a gaping hole as Humphrey cleared it. The first descent was less than a man's height, down a short and far from safe wooden ladder. The atmosphere at the bottom of it was a unique combination —of damp earth, damp lime—and cheese: about a dozen and a half seven-pounders were standing on wooden racks that had empty space for a good many more.

'When did you last turn those buggers?' Septimus wanted to know.

'They're due for turning at the end of the week,' Humphrey told him. 'Do you want me to do it now?'

'Don't be so thick-headed. And don't give me any of your

bloody lip. Do you think Mr Brunt wants us down here at
this time of night to turn cheeses?'

Humphrey's only reaction was a bovine stolidity. Beyond
the space used for storage, a broad flight of stone steps led
downwards and away into darkness. Brunt's torch was not
strong enough for him to see where it led, but he could make
out rough-hewn walls on either side, covered in patches with
a rippling stalagmatic deposit, glistening with moisture and
stained by the mineral deposits that were carried in solution
in the water. Here and there water was falling from the roof
in fine, steady pencils.

'I see no sign of any worked-out vein,' Brunt said.

'There isn't one up here. This was only the Old Man's
way in. There's no showing of ore for at least fifty yards.'

'How the blazes did he know he'd find it when he got
there, then?'

'That was something he could never be certain of. He was
a worker, was the Old Man. And he always lived in hope.'

Septimus held his lantern to try to see further down, but
the adit bore into a right-hand curve, beyond which there
was no seeing.

'He'll have had a rough idea too from the way the veins
lie in the hill above us. He was a long-headed bugger, was
the Old Man. I've heard it said he had an extra sense, when
he was looking for lead. If he made a mistake, he might
have to go on drilling for weeks without earning. That
happened to him often enough. Right, Mr Brunt—you'd
better let me go first—and watch it on those steps. They're
slippery, they're uneven, and they peter out after the first
couple of dozen or so. After that, there's only one safe way
down, and that's going to be on our arses. You come last,
Humphrey. Bring the rope and tackle.'

It was as Septimus said. The steps were not only treacherous, they felt treacherous. This was no public staircase.
Stone slabs of roughly the right size and shape had been
brought here as found, laid down and crudely wedged as

best suited the lie of the floor in any particular place. They were not uniform in width and were greasy with a coating of water-borne mud.

'See what we're coming to?

Septimus stopped and held his lantern above his head.

'Up to now we've been in the Old Man's trial boring. Round about here he struck into a natural cavity. He was always hoping to do that. It could save him a lot of backache. In another few yards you'll see where slickensides starts.'

And it was so. Septimus showed Brunt the shiny surface —or, at least, a surface that would be a good deal shinier than it was if someone were to wash it clean of the encrustations of centuries. But lateral grooves were clearly visible where two opposing rock-faces had been dragged past each other under the immense pressure of the geological fault. Over one oval patch, the surface rock had splintered away.

'Somebody had a narrow escape when that cracked,' Septimus said. 'Slickensides is treacherous. As Humphrey once discovered.'

Humphrey said nothing.

Here was the end of the flight of steps. Below the last of them the ground curved down and away, like the lower slopes of a mountain strewn with scree. Septimus drew Brunt's attention to a tapering gap in the roof above them.

'That's what I was telling you about—the *deads*—the waste stone from the working. Up there, out of the Old Man's way, stowed on old timber. If you were to fire a shotgun in here, the reverberation could be enough to bring it down. See that corner—I'll swear there's been a fall from there since I was last in here. Bloody tons of it. And it's down on our bums from now on, Mr Brunt. It's not going to do your suit all that much good. You'll have to slither. And try not to stub your toes against anything that might shift. There's no telling what we might set in motion.'

In point of fact the next part of the way down was not as difficult as it had looked at first sight. The gradient was less

steep than it had looked in the impenetrable shadows cast
by their lamps. Brunt lowered himself on the flat of his
hands, feeling gingerly forward with his feet. Then Septimus
held out a warning hand to stop him from coming down
further.

'God! I know now what you've been talking about. I've
never known water held here like this. Come down beside
me—slowly—take care—you'll see what I mean.'

Brunt moved cautiously down to him and Septimus threw
a pebble ahead of them. It splashed into deep water, waking
a series of weird distant echoes.

'Up there to the left is the waterswallow. It's rare for
there to be a regular flow down there—just a few hundred
gallons a day in wet weather. Normally its a fairly easy
climb down there—bit of a tight fit, but that saves you from
slipping. But I've never known anybody who's been down
and talked about a pool at the bottom like this.'

'You told me the lower parts were badly flooded.'

'I tell everybody that. It keeps the nosey buggers out.
There's deep flooding in one of the lower galleries, where
the Old Man had to give up working—but that's a long
way from here.'

'What happens to the water that normally runs down
here? It must be coming in from more places than one.'

'It comes in at dozens of places, from all over the hillside.
But it all runs away. Some of it feeds the Cotter Spring, for
one thing. No wonder it's dry. Nothing's getting through.'

Septimus had become more and more civil as he saw that
the story about the Cotter Spring was more than a rumour.

'How's it getting away from here to flood Brindley's
clough?' Brunt asked.

'It isn't, as far as I can see. It looks to me as if it's standing
still.'

Brunt could not see the whole extent of the standing
pool, which was flanked on one side by the outfall of the
waterswallow and on the other by a bank of stones and clay.

Beyond that was another gulf of dense blackness in which they could hear water dripping in many places, the drips in cross-rhythm with each other.

'How far can one get past there?' Brunt asked Septimus.

'A long way. Walking to your full height, too. There are chambers down there you could lose my farmhouse in, yard and all. Till you come to the flood, further down.'

'You've seen all this for yourself?'

'Years ago.'

'Another Wonder of the Peak—something not many people have ever set eyes on.'

'Something not many even know about.'

'What's it like underfoot?'

'Wet and rocky. Mucky, too.'

'No chance of it ever being opened up to the public?'

Septimus turned and stared at him for a long time without speaking.

'I'd ideas in that direction once,' he said at last. 'But it would need more than one man's working lifetime to make it fit for visitors.'

He got to his feet, picked his way down to the edge of the water, then scrambled some way up the bank that was acting as a dam on the right hand side.

'The rain pelted down once or twice the night before last. That's your answer, Mr Brunt. If there were enough to raise the level here another three inches, you can see where the overflow would get through. And some of it could find its way to Brindley's.'

He did not come back to Brunt immediately, but pottered about where he was, shifting a stone in one place, testing the firmness of another.

'How deep would you say it is, Septimus?'

'About eight feet at its deepest—that's at the far end.'

'And that's where it generally runs out to Cotter's?'

'Yes—but there's nothing to show for it down there—it isn't a watercourse in the normal sense: just loose stones that it trickles down through. Sometimes you can hear the water under them—but you can't see it.'

'So what could be blocking it? A roof fall?'

'I don't see that that could do it. There'd be too many gaps, unless it was mixed with enough mud to bind it. Water will find its way through where it can.'

'How big an area would have to be blocked off?'

'Dunno. Couple of square yards, maybe.'

'Didn't I once hear of a dead sheep stopping up a water-course?'

'It's been known—but there's no way a sheep could get down here.'

'No—but a man could, couldn't he? A man's body, perhaps with a tumble of rubble on top of it?'

Septimus looked rancorously at the pool.

'I'm not bloody well going in there to see.'

'I'm not asking you to. What is there past the bank? How deep is it down the other side?'

'It falls away thirty feet or so.'

'Have you a hose about the farm?'

Septimus saw at once what Brunt had in mind.

'Humphrey, go and get the hose-pipe—the long one, from the cart-shed.'

Humphrey did not say anything. He turned, his shoulders sagging, and clambered up the slope on his hands and knees. They heard his iron-shod heels ringing on the stone steps above.

'Now, Septimus,' Brunt said. 'Is there anything you feel you ought to be telling me?'

'Me? What are you trying to pin on me, Mr Brunt?'

'I think you can work out for yourself what the odds are. Who are we going to find down there, do you reckon?'

'Are you accusing me of something, Mr Brunt?'

'I'm asking you to tell me anything you think I ought to know.'

'Do you think that if I'd had anything to do with drowning

a man down here, I'd have brought you here the way I have?'

'You might,' Brunt said.

'Who do you think it is, then?'

'I'm asking you. Let me put it another way—who's gone missing from Walderslow? We both know the answer to that, don't we?'

Brunt pulled himself laboriously to his feet and did what Durden had done—lowered himself to the edge of the water and shone his torch at it. It gleamed back at him from the blackness.

'Yes: it should be possible to siphon it off, Septimus—with your cooperation.'

'You want my cooperation? So you can nail the blame on me?'

'The best way of not blaming the wrong man is to make sure we get the right one.'

Then they heard a thundering noise above them, something foreign to the mine—a loud hollow banging that echoed resonantly above and all round them.

'Christ! That bloody idiot is putting the floorboards back. He's for trapping us down here and buggering off!'

Septimus rushed like a madman up the slope, falling once on his knees and ignoring the hurt that he had obviously done himself. But he was too late at the top of the steps— in time to hear his son dragging and throwing heavy objects over their only way out.

CHAPTER 7

Charlotte Machin knew from experience how an overnight resolve could weaken by morning. She knew what it was to go to bed with determination on her mind, only to wake up with it sour on her palate. She remembered how once years ago Horatio had reprimanded her and she had made up her mind in the bravery of her bedroom to make him withdraw what he said—or she would leave his employ.

It was one of those infrequent occasions when he had impinged tangentially on the life of the nursery. Barnard had told a lie to escape some minor trouble and she had punished him by sending him to bed with a bread-and-water supper. She had never understood how Horatio had learned of the incident, but he had intervened and Barnard had told him a spur-of-the-moment false front story. His father brought him downstairs and told him to get anything he wanted from the larder. The boy had passed Miss Machin with a triumphant grin and a tray loaded with boiled ham, a chicken wing, cold potatoes and apple pie. She had lain awake rehearsing the next morning's dialogue, but when the morning came she had had nothing to say. The situation resolved itself because Horatio had forgotten the whole incident, reverting to his usual condition of not knowing what was going on in the life of his household.

But today, a couple of hours before the dawn, when she ought, according to all the norms, to have been sinking at last into a quasi delirious sleep, she was wider awake than ever. She felt—a danger signal if ever there was one—no sense of fatigue. She got out of bed and began packing her valise—two changes of underclothing, two longcloth nightdresses, woollen drawers and vests, a lighter costume for the spring days that must surely come: there was much she would have to leave behind. Or perhaps when the first shock had subsided, she would write to Horatio and ask him to have her other things sent on. Cook, or Mrs Durden, who came in once a week to do the laundry, could pack them all up for her. Charlotte Machin had not thought anything out, was incapable of thinking properly here and now. Grasshopperwise she leaped from one activity to another, feverishly checked the balance in her Penny Savings Bank passbook. Horatio paid her the appalling pittance of eighteen pounds a year, about which she had never argued with him. In fact she hardly spent more than a third of that and believed she had put enough by in twenty years to keep herself comfortable for the winter. She did not think ahead of next spring.

She would be out of the house before Horatio was up. She would go to the village carrying her own bag, braving the insolent wonderment of anyone she met, would go to Henry Drabble and hire his carriage to take her to the railway. There would be no looking back over her shoulder.

Horatio Brittlebank's sleeplessness took a different form, a falling in and out of surrealistic dozes.

He too had decided to be out of the house early in the morning—early at any rate for him. A mundane but pervasively satisfying solution had entered his brain. He would go and talk to Mr Bailey, his solicitor in Buxton. Mr Bailey was a man of quiet and assuring common sense and efficiency. He would know how to contact his son in Canada. Brittlebank had made the great mental step of convincing himself that what was needed at this juncture was a generous gesture. The boy had his mother's inheritance, but God knew how much of that he had dissipated at Oxford. Perhaps an offer of some advance settlement on the Walderslow estate—in exchange, of course, for relieving him of the cares of management—would bring him home. The word *bribe* did not enter into Brittlebank's considerations, but he was man of the world enough to admit to himself that peace of mind sometimes had to be paid for; peace of mind presupposing an assurance that nothing would change in any aspect of his life.

He was out of his bed by seven-thirty—an hour and a half before his usual time, and his first impression was that the house seemed unusually cold. And surely Miss Machin was usually up and about by now? The thought did not enter his head that there was likely to be any prolonged estrangement because of the way he had spoken to her last night: that had only been in the distress of the moment.

He went along the landing with the intention of knocking on Miss Machin's door—he needed, among other things, his shaving water. But when he reached her door, he found that it was standing half open. He did not dare to look round it: he felt there was a strong element of anathema about a woman's bedroom—even Miss Machin's. He said her name, not loudly, and there was no reply. He called more vigorously, but Miss Machin had already gone.

He went down to the kitchen to get his hot water himself, found that room as chilly as the rest of the Hall, no fire lit, even yesterday's ashes not raked out.

Harlow and Topliss were also out of bed early, despite the late hour at which they had retired from Harlow's attempts to school his companion for Monte Carlo. Both men were capable of burning the candle at both ends. At more than one critical moment in their life together, their survival had depended on that ability.

Harlow knocked on Topliss's door, went in without ceremony and shook his assistant urgently by the shoulder.

'Come on. We have to look lively. I'll dig Bramwell out and have him fry us a breakfast. Go round to that man Drabble and make sure he has his trap here in an hour's time. They'll be expecting us to leave today—but I want them to find that we've gone.'

Septimus ran up the scree like a man demented, without assistance from his hands or arms, springing forward on the balls of his feet as another man would have run along the flat. Then he clattered up the stone-slab steps and Brunt heard him thumping with some iron instrument at the floorboards under which they were trapped. It was obviously to no avail. Durden shouted up at the timbers, a mouthful of tumbling obscenities. Doubtless they brought him some relief, but the only response was an echo.

Brunt sat patiently and switched off his torch to save the battery. The life of the mine came at him in a torrent of sound from all directions: water dripping into water, water dripping on to rock, water flowing, water lapping against stone. And there were other sounds in dark unseen places, for which it was not easy to imagine any cause: a small stone falling for no discernible reason, at what seemed a great distance away. It was not surprising that unquestioned legends had grown up in the mining villages. Brunt heard sounds in a remote gallery that most lonely listeners would be tempted to identify as footsteps—footsteps that seemed for ever to be receding, and yet that paradoxically never went anywhere. The Old Man, walking his sough, arching his back under one of his thin, penurious workings?

Brunt saw the rays of Durden's lamp shine round the curve in the adit as he came back down, casting living shadows that moved round the cavern like erratic hours on a mad sundial. Durden was shouting with rage as he came and stood by the spot where Brunt was sitting.

'That bloody woman! She knows bloody well we're down here. I told her I was bringing you down. And she'll not have missed a trick. She'll know that good-for-nothing bloody jack o'lantern son of mine has shut us in.'

'Then she's bound to let us out sooner or later,' Brunt said quietly, apparently totally unmoved by any sense of danger, physical discomfort or even minor inconvenience. 'Perhaps she's gone back to bed.'

'It wouldn't surprise me. You don't know that bloody woman. She'll not let us out till she feels like it. Ten to one she thinks she's teaching me some sort of lesson.'

He swung his lamp, looking round himself for something violent to do. He was a man for whom violence was a necessity when he was opposed, a man who needed to be doing something, however futile, when he was up against it. He went down again now to the edge of the water, got across to the bank on its right-hand edge and began to test the stones to see if there were any that he could dislodge.

But he did not find one that would oblige him by shifting under his not inconsiderable strength. Then he thought of something else, went bounding back up to the entrance and came back with a long, rusted crowbar, probably the thing he had used to hammer the floorboards with. He took it down to the bank, found a spot where he could insert it under one of the large lower stones, drove it in as far as he could and worked on it with all the leverage that his muscle-power could apply. Brunt could see that he was summoning up every latent ounce of his strength, glorying in the challenge, but still he could not get anything to budge. He stood, balancing miraculously, on the protruding edge of the crowbar, jumped up and down on it.

And suddenly something happened—or began to happen. There was a crack. He jumped off the bar and applied more leverage. It sounded as if a stone was splitting; then its neighbour shifted. For an instant the bank seemed poised on the verge of collapse. Then it did collapse—or, at least, a substantial portion of it did. It fell in an avalanche down the thirty-foot drop to the series of great chambers of which he had spoken. He helped more of the wall on its way with his hands, clawing at the unwieldy boulders with a strength that he surely only possessed when he was enraged. He got his arms round one great stone, rocked it as a dentist might begin to loosen a deeply embedded molar. Brunt sat as placid and unmoved as if he were watching a game of bowls. And then the keystone went, undermining the bank.

The noise was thunderous as the falling stones set lower accumulations of rubble in motion. Brunt looked up involuntarily at the great piles of working waste stowed away on dubious timbers in the roof. Could all this vibration be enough to bring that lot down? Mercifully, it appeared to be holding good.

But what was happening now was that the water in the pool was emptying itself out fast, the way the debris of the bank had gone. It was as if one side of a tank were suddenly removed. There was a sluicing, sucking noise and water cascaded away without grace or ceremony, leaving not more than a foot remaining below the outfall level—water opaque with glutinous mud. And at the far end, where Durden had estimated the depth at eight feet, lay a man's body, face downwards, the head furthest from the two men, the shoulders weighted down by half a dozen stones the size of hams.

Both men went down to the corpse, squelching through mud almost up to their knees, neither of them considering the soaking cold. They both worked at casting the impedimenta aside from the man's back. They both put a hand to a shoulder to turn the body face upwards.

Face? There was not a feature to be recognized. Apart from the filth with which they were plastered, cheeks, nose and eye-sockets were stove in by battering against rock. The jaw had been crushed.

'Is that young Brittlebank?' Brunt wanted to know. 'Remember, I never met him.'

'It's him all right—though I don't know who's going to identify him for you from that mess. I can tell from his build and the cut of his cloth. I've seen him in those clothes—and there's none but a Brittlebank in Walderslow would be wearing custom-built brown boots.'

Already, now they had moved the head, there was a bubbling of water as the rest of it was beginning to find its normal channel to the Cotter Spring.

'We don't have to hang over him, do we?' Durden asked. 'Christ! I thought I had a strong gut!'

They went back to the foot of the scree, where Brunt had been sitting most of the time.

'Well—there's nothing we can do for *him*,' Durden said.

'Except find out how he comes to be lying there in that state.'

'That's not going to help him much, is it?'

'Maybe not. But it's any dead man's right to be investigated. So I'm asking you again, Septimus. Is there anything you're itching to tell me?'

'I'm as smock-raffled as you are, Mr Brunt. I see no reason behind it.'

'No? Is there nobody who thinks he has good reason for having it in for Barnard Brittlebank? Is there nothing you think you ought to start telling me about your lad, for example?'

'Nay. He'll have had nothing to do with this. He hasn't got it in him.'

'No? Do you know what I'm thinking, Septimus?'

'Nay, Mr Brunt. There's many a man would have given a fortune in his time to have known the answer to that.'

'I'm thinking that it may not be to teach you a lesson that your dear lady wife has shut us up down here.'

'I take no responsibility for anything that's going on in that woman's head.'

'Don't you think, Septimus, she may be giving your beloved son a little time in which to put some distance between himself and me?'

'I don't like the way your mind works at all, Mr Brunt. If you knew the very first thing about that soft lad of mine, such an idea wouldn't enter your head.'

'Well, it has entered my head, and it's still there. So you can help us while the time away by telling me how much your Humphrey ever had to do with young Brittlebank.'

'That'll not take long. I won't pretend that the two of them were friends. They've had nothing to do with each other for years.'

'I did hear that they sometimes went about together in their younger days.'

'They went together once, Mr Brunt—and that's something my Humphrey will not forget to his dying day. Because

I came down heavy on him for what he did—very heavy. I'm going to tell you about that, then you'll not get hold of the wrong end of the story from anybody else. It isn't a story that anybody else knows—but that doesn't stop them from trying to tell it. I've not told the inside of it to a soul in my life—but I'm going to tell it you now.'

He settled himself down beside Brunt, making himself as comfortable as the stones would allow.

'I gave that boy the thrashing of his life—and I've never regretted it. I'll admit I had to hold myself back from killing him, and that was after I'd waited a fortnight for the pleasure. Or, let's say, for the duty. It was a duty, Mr Brunt. And it was because he'd given away a family secret. He took Barnard Brittlebank, and Bill Cartledge's lad, shifted the top-stone and brought them down the waterswallow, to where we are now, took them over the bank that I just pushed over, showed them some of the caverns that lie down there. Those are my treasures, Mr Brunt—*were* my treasures. Humphrey showed them a curtain of stalactites, not a one of them broken or chipped, that I'll wager you won't see matched anywhere in the world. There are waterfalls, splashing over rocks coloured all the hues of the rainbow. I'd taken the lad down there on his twelfth birthday, and I don't know that there were two other people on the face of the earth that day who'd ever seen what I showed him.'

'So why all the secrecy, Septimus?'

'Because those sights were my treasure. It only wanted opening up—a few dangerous stacks of rubble shoring up, handrails fixed, footpaths squared up. It's been my ambition to make a public showpiece of it: I've done some of the work, a bit at a time. Those steps at the top—the ones we came down—they were my work: the Old Man went to his seam without that kind of convenience. But there's been a limit to what I could do: I've had a farm to run, cheese to make and sell, at one time beer to brew. I was waiting for

Humphrey to grow up. He'd have helped me—and had the income from it.'

'You keep talking in the past tense, Septimus.'

'It is all in the past—now.'

'Why should it be?'

'Because I've lost it. Because I had three bad years on the trot: foot and mouth through the herd, milk at what I had to give for it, cheese trade lost and never made up. I'd have lost my farm, if I hadn't gone to Brittlebank for a loan. But he wouldn't give me one, wouldn't hear of a mortgage on Slickensides. All he would do—and I was pressed, Mr Brunt—was buy Middle Furlong, and now I have to pay him a peppercorn rental for the right to cross my own field.'

'But as land it was no great loss to you, I'd have thought.'

'You think not? We're under Middle Furlong at this moment, Mr Brunt. If I were fool enough to try to make a living from this mine, the royalty would be payable to Brittlebank now: he's the landowner; his are the mineral rights now. What the Barmote Court calls the Lord's Seam: I'd have to work it for him. And if anybody ever opens those caverns up to the public, it'll be Barnard Brittlebank. Now you know why somebody's nicking my stowe—why somebody wants my mine. And who will that be? Who would it be but Barnard Brittlebank? Who the hell else could have an interest in owning Slickensides?'

'Why should Barnard Brittlebank want the bother of opening a showpiece cavern? He wouldn't want the work and he doesn't need the money.'

'He'd like to think he was depriving someone else of it.'

'So you think it was he who broke into your creamery?'

'Him or somebody working for him.'

'Which doesn't put you in a very promising relationship with him, does it, Septimus—with murder on the bill of fare?'

'What I've told you is the truth, Mr Brunt. You'll have

to make of it what you see fit. But it doesn't make me the killer of the man—or Humphrey either.'

'Nothing would please me more than to take you at your word, Septimus. I hope it works out that way. You know what my job is, and you know me well enough to know that I shall be doing my best at it. And I don't see how you can speak for what your son's been up to. It's well known that you and he are not the best of friends, and you can't account for every minute of his time.'

'Every minute of his time is spent on the farm.'

'While you're in the Pig? While you're sleeping off your Saturday morning ale?'

Durden became silent, got up and walked aimlessly about, but never disappearing from Brunt's sight. It was fully half an hour before he came back and sat down again.

'You said something very true, earlier on, Mr Brunt. You said—or at least that's what you meant—that the only thing that'll help me is for me to find out who did do it. I reckon I stand a better chance of doing that than you do. People won't know what I'm grafting at. I'll have them off their guard. If you see me doing one or two things that look a bit queer—can I trust you not to interfere?'

Brunt gave that some thought.

'Within reason,' he said at last. 'But no promises. I'm accountable to bigger people than myself. There's no telling what they're going to demand. They might think the Brittlebanks cut enough ice to deserve attention from men senior to me.'

'Have you the time on you, Mr Brunt?'

Brunt pulled out a heavy-duty timepiece.

'Half past three.'

'Ellen gets up at five. God knows how long after that before she gives up this caper.'

The next stretch of the night was long. There was no comfort in the mine, there was no silence. After paddling in the filth of the pool both men were miserable in their clothes.

Durden moved stones about, cleared himself an area where he could lie approximately flat, showing as little sign of outward torture as if he were lying in straw. He stopped talking and there was no sound from him but his breathing. Brunt did not know whether he was asleep or not.

Durden had turned down the wick of his lamp to the nearest bud. Brunt wondered how much oil was left in its reservoir. He switched his own torch off again. There was only the faintest glimmer now by which he could see the stones nearest to him. The impoverished flame of the lantern could not reach the walls. Brunt sat with his knees up, his elbows across them, supporting his chin. He dozed off unrestfully time after time, woke abruptly whenever his head fell forward. He tried to make systematic plans for all that had to be done tomorrow. He had to report to his office. There would be an inquest on Barnard Brittlebank to be arranged. A post mortem report on a dog had to be collected. He had to start a search for information about the background of Harvey Harlow and Topliss. He had to find some way of keeping the two Londoners in Walderslow. He had to question the members of the Durden family in depth and at length; and perhaps he would have to talk to William Cartledge, who might be a source of information without bias. He had to start a hue and cry for Humphrey Durden, and would probably have to direct it himself. This was one of those cases that would have long-lasting ramifications if it were not solved almost immediately.

It was shortly before six that the mine began to echo to unearthly rumblings in its upper reaches. There were sounds of heavy obstructions being pulled off the floorboards, then the raising of the timber above them a plank at a time. New light shone down, and Ellen Durden's wiry and resolute figure stood looking down at them from above. She did not come further than the bottom of the steps.

'Good morning, gentlemen—I trust you passed a comfortable night?'

Brunt simply switched on his torch and shone it on Barnard Brittlebank's corpse for her benefit.

'My God!'

'So where is your son, Mrs Durden? With your connivance he's half way across northern England by now, I shouldn't wonder.'

'He's in the yard, getting ready for the milking.'

CHAPTER 8

There is a constant temperature in underground places in Derbyshire, about 52 degrees Fahrenheit, give or take a chilling draught or two. Consequently mines and caves are comparatively warm places in winter, and cool when the sun is shining outside. Brunt knew this well enough, but he was taken by surprise by the cold clamminess of the air as they came out through the creamery into the yard. A thick mist had come down during the night and angles of wall loomed out of it, spectral and incomplete. It was impossible to see as far as the farmhouse. The prospects dismayed Brunt. If this were to develop into the sort of hill-fog that the region could produce in its more spiteful hours, the day's work was going to demand a Hercules.

For all her jeering attitude Ellen Durden invited Brunt into her kitchen for tea and oatcakes.

'I'm in no fit state to come into a woman's kitchen,' he said, with little show of courtesy. 'And we've work to do before I think of anything else.'

He said we've, and Septimus did not question that he was going to work alongside Brunt until the essentials were behind them. He found an old warped and rotting barn door on which, with many mishaps and difficulties, they eventually hauled Barnard Brittlebank's body up the slope and the adit. They carried the corpse into one of the sheds.

Ellen Durden helped them with the extempore stretcher. She had been startled by her first sight of the dead man, but rapidly became accustomed to him, exhibited no revulsion, and obviously took pride in her aggressive lack of femininity.

When the task was done, she again asked Brunt in for something to eat and drink, but he declined again, clearly in the spirit of a man who was going to accept no hospitality until the divisions between ally and enemy were plainer to see.

'It isn't a crime to offer a pot of tea,' she said.

'No. But obstruction's a crime—though I might just happen to forget being shut up for the night, if I could be sure of cooperation from now on.'

'And who isn't cooperating?'

'Someone who killed a man down there,' Brunt said.

'A man's had a nasty accident. I could see that. We don't know yet that anybody killed him, do we?'

'No. We don't know. We still think he might have got up with his face mangled and his head agape, climbed to the top, pulled the floorboards back over himself, then gone back down to lie face downwards in the water.'

For the first time, she looked abashed.

'I see what you mean, Mr Brunt.'

'So you'll also see, I hope, what I must be thinking about your Humphrey.'

'I've given Humphrey a piece of my mind. You'll have no more trouble from him.'

'He's been behaving very like a guilty young man, according to my book.'

'Like a frightened one, you mean—a frightened young fool. He hasn't the slightest idea what happened down there —his only thought was that he'd be blamed for it—as he takes the blame for everything that ever goes wrong on Slickensides. That's why he tried to make off—though where he thinks he would have gone, God only knows. I've talked some sense into him. He'll do his best to tell you anything you want to know—but it won't be much, because he doesn't know much.'

'I'll be back to see him—and you others too. I'm going up to Ted Milward's now, to get myself dry clothes.'

'When you do come to talk to Humphrey, don't expect miracles, Mr Brunt. He's no speech-maker.'

'I've been known to make good sense out of a row of yeas and nays, Mrs Durden.'

'It would be better if I were with you when you talked to him. I can get answers out of him when others can't.'

'I'll bear that in mind if I get stuck,' Brunt said, but he did not sound as if he meant it.

He let himself out of the outside gate. Away from the house the fog was thick. It was impossible to see across the road to the opposite verge.

Horatio Brittlebank stood and shivered in the cold and inhospitable kitchen, then went back across his huge entrance hall and up the broad staircase, calling Miss Machin. No answer came.

This time he did knock on her open door, and after a discreet pause looked round it. She was not there. Her bed had been stripped to the mattress. A wardrobe door had been opened and not closed again. He saw with distaste a few small and unnamable articles of female clothing scattered about the floor: he had always thought she was a tidy woman.

He went up and down this and other landings, calling her again. What the blazes did she think she was playing at? He had been a little short with her last night, he admitted to himself. He always resented it when she tried to insinuate herself into his business at times of crisis. It was almost as if she regarded herself as a member of his family.

He went back down to the kitchen. Cook would not be in till nine, though Albert Clayton, his coachman and general

handyman, was supposed to be at work by eight: Brittlebank
had for a long time suspected that with his master still abed,
Clayton was keeping hours to suit himself.

Brittlebank's fingers discovered the bristles on his chin.
A man unshaven was a man unfit to face the day. It was
beginning to dawn on him that today was going to be one
of the worst he had ever lived through.

He was uncertain where to look for kindling and coals,
but found them at last and half an hour later had still not
got the fire going.

Henry Drabble was still at his breakfast when Topliss
knocked at his door. He was taking his time, eating oatcakes
fried in pork dripping, topped with fried potatoes and swilled
down with prodigious quantities of strong tea. The moment
he had looked out of his window this morning, he had known
that he could afford a day of expansive leisure.

He knew Topliss and disliked him. He knew him because
he had driven him and Harlow up and down the countryside
from one stable to another, the day they were supposed to
be investigating Barnard Brittlebank's departure from the
village. He disliked him because he saw him as what he was
—Harlow's dogsbody. That was something that Topliss did
not care for others to see through, preferring to present
himself as a clever man's intellectual companion. And when
not accompanied by the clever man, he was inclined to
assume the maestro's role himself. He had not fooled anyone
in Walderslow, Henry Drabble least of all.

'Servants usually use the back door,' Drabble said, without getting up from the table—or even swallowing what he
was in the process of masticating.

'It's just that we want a carriage to Buxton Station in an
hour's time.'

'Which you won't be getting.'

'If you have other engagements, Mr Harlow wants me to
say that—'

'Do you know what it's like over the tops this morning?
I shan't be putting a horse in the shafts today, and nor won't
anyone else who's in his right mind.'

'I'm sure Mr Harlow would make it worth—'

'Make it worth while breaking a horse's leg, and two
wheels in the ditch? We should be off the road before we
were a quarter of a mile out of Walderslow.'

'Later on today, then, perhaps—?'

'There won't be any later on today. This could hang
about for a week. If you don't care for a blindfold walk to
the turnpike, you'll have to make do with the pleasures of
the Pig. And now, if you'll kindly leave a man in peace at
his table—'

Charlotte Machin rarely went into Walderslow—as rarely
as she could manage, and certainly never on foot if she could
help it. Cook, who lived in the village, did most of the
household shopping, but now and then there was something
that Miss Machin did not care to depute to anyone. When
she was in Walderslow, she never allowed herself to be
drawn into conversation and she distanced herself so obviously from people that *toffee-nosed* was the adjective that she
naturally attracted. It did not occur to the villagers that she
might be afraid of them, afraid of her own inability to
communicate with the class of men and women with whom
she had been brought up.

Without breakfast, and surprised by the weight of her
valise, she set out from the Hall, consciously avoiding the
error of Lot's wife. Never before had she been in the village
as early in the morning as this, except for dawn journeys
through it in a carriage when the Brittlebanks were catching
an early train. She had not expected the rawness of this
November morning. Close to the walls of the Hall, she could
still make out the lines and corners of the building, but away
from the relative warmth of the house, the hill mists reduced
visibility to a ten-yard radius. She had to abandon her

original notion of crossing the fields, where she felt it less likely that she would make any chance encounters, and had to take to the road, which added a mile to the distance. Two workmen, on their way to the quarries at Hindlow, tramped past her, figures that she could not even see in the white, choking blanket. She was petrified by their approach, was afraid of what they might say to her. They grunted something in their coarse dialect. She assumed that it was an impudence—though they were not able to see her, either.

She had to set down her bag and change hands, had to do that again and again at increasingly short intervals over the next hundred yards, her fingers cramped like bloodless claws. A dip in the road was the beginning of an upward gradient and the cold damp air was beginning to sear into her lungs.

Up here the mist seemed denser than ever, and she could see it moving past her in impenetrable strands. The eddies looked at some moments as if they might part, and she prayed that they would thin out so that she could see where she was. But just whenever her hopes were raised, the curtain seemed to come together again. Her eyes ached with trying to see through it.

She set down her case again, realizing for the first time that she was all-in after her night without sleep. Her eyes burned and a persistent pain was troubling the back of her neck. Also she was beginning to wish that she had forced herself to have something to eat before leaving the house: her stomach felt sick with emptiness. Persistent and irrational images began to torture her brain. She saw a small boy of eight or nine in a painted iron bath-tub, could smell the steam from the water, the wholesome carbolic soap—that Horatio was always complaining about. She sensed the comfort of towels warming on a clothes-horse in front of a coal fire. It was so many years ago: she hated the memory of that scene, wanted to shriek at it to go away, but it continued to haunt her. Something black and formless lurched at her from the side of the road, made her actually utter a little squeal. It was a sheep.

She came to a crossroads, only recognized it as such because she had started walking with the hem of her skirt brushing against the grasses at the edge of the road. This, she had told herself, was rather a clever way of making sure that she did not go off course.

She thought it was the crossroads where a bridle-path to Hartington branched off in one direction, and the lane to Walderslow downhill to her left. This was the way that she must take and she left the protective verge, feeling, when she reached the middle of the road, as if she were irretrievably lost without sense of direction in an impermeable cold, white universe. Five minutes later her ankle doubled up under her in a hole in the ground. It was not actually sprained, but the pain was enough to make her stop and rest. She knew now that she had left the road behind, that she had somehow got on to a track that had tapered down to nothing in the middle of a rough field. She knew she had no hope of finding her way back to the crossroads. She told herself that if she could only compel herself to keep going in a straight line, she was bound to come presently to a habitation and people. She did not know that the human tendency, when wandering about in open space as she was, was almost always to go round in repetitive circles.

'How long is this going to persist, Ted?'

'Perhaps it'll begin to thin out about tea-time—an hour or so before it starts to get dark. Then it'll come down again in the night. Once this lot starts, it can go on for a week or two at this time of year.'

'Nothing could serve me worse,' Brunt said. 'If I don't get in touch with Derby somehow—if I can't get inquiries started in London—this whole lot's going to run away with me.'

There was no telephone in Walderslow. Nobody so far had

wanted the expense—nobody thought his sort of business warranted it. Some men were frightened of being in such close touch with the active world. In the normal run of his rural cases, Brunt made great use of the railway telegraph, but he had just pointed out that if he tried to walk to Parsley Hay or Dowlow under these conditions, there was every likelihood he would find himself cut off from everybody, unable even to get back to Walderslow. Then where would they be?

Milward was a much bigger man than Brunt, and could fill out the old jacket that now hung about Brunt's shoulders like something on a scarecrow. And he was only able to wear a pair of Milward's trousers by turning up ten inches at the bottom of the legs, and having the crotch hang halfway down to his knees. No one in the Milward household saw anything funny in his appearance.

Bessie Milward had cooked him a pantagruelian breakfast, which he was now eating. She was a bonny, active, warm-smiling woman who during her husband's duty life had almost been part of the police force herself, passing messages, setting distressed people's minds at rest and sometimes even spotting before Ted did the sinister discrepancy that had brought some country wrongdoer to book.

'At least, one good thing has come out of it,' Brunt said, glancing at the thick vapours outside the window. 'I don't see Harlow and Topliss getting out of Walderslow either. Henry Drabble won't harness up today, that's for certain. I don't want that pair out of my reach—and I haven't enough to hold them on.'

'I should have thought that you had,' Milward said. 'They spread those lies about Barnard Brittlebank going to Canada, didn't they? That's what they came here for, isn't it? Surely that's involvement enough.'

'Maybe they didn't think it was a lie. Maybe they believed it was the truth they'd been sent here to tell. You can be sure that's the way they'd tell it to a magistrate—and be believed.'

He stuck his fork into a crisp corner of fried bread.

'Maybe we're not going to find the answer to any of this in Walderslow. Oxford, London—those places are a long way away—busy places. And Barnard Brittlebank has travelled half way across Europe, this last year. Somebody'll have to put feelers out all over the globe. And I can't even get a message to Buxton, six miles away.'

Mrs Ada Harrison, who had cooked for Horatio Brittlebank for the last seventeen years, had no great love for him. It was out of a dogged sense of life's continuities, together with a habit of always doing what she had said she would do, that she set off for Walderslow Hall at her usual time. But first she called at Maggie Thwaites's shop for bacon, knowing that supplies were running low in Brittlebank's larder.

So far she did not see the difficulties ahead of her. Where there were domestic walls, there was domestic warmth, and even a degree or two of higher temperature was enough to relieve the opacity in the village street. But after she had passed the Methodist Chapel, the last outpost on that side of Walderslow, she suddenly found that she had quite unintentionally crossed to the opposite side of the road. Then she was almost run down by a brave man with a cart who had ventured out on an errand from a farmyard to a field-gate less than a furlong away. She wheezed, thought unladylike thoughts, but continued on her route undeterred.

There came, however, a moment of incipient fear when the thought struck her that she had lost track of how far she had come along her route. There was a lane into which she had to turn to reach the Hall—the same lane, coming from the opposite direction—into which Charlotte Machin had mistakenly believed she was turning—and Ada Harrison did not know whether she had missed it or not. A terrible new fear struck her—and it was not that she was going to get lost along a three-mile lane that she had trodden some twelve thousand times in the service of the Brittlebanks. What began to eat into her soul was that she was going to be late, which would mean having to face a caustic Miss Machin and a sullen Mr Brittlebank. Horatio Brittlebank was not a man to make allowances for the elements, especially elements hidden from his sight (and imagination) by manorial walls.

It was when Ada Harrison stumbled over a milestone that proclaimed her to be only two miles from Pilsbury that she stood still and wept. In seventeen years and twelve thousand journeys, she had never penetrated as far along this by-road as this—she was not a native of Walderslow. Now she was going to be unthinkably late.

Ada Harrison was not an intelligent woman, merely a creature steered by familiar rhythms. When those rhythms were callously broken, she was apt to give up thinking altogether. She turned and decided to go home—still clutching Horatio Brittlebank's bacon. It took her rather longer to get back to her cottage than it might have done to reach Walderslow Hall.

But at least she was saved from the dudgeon in which her employer was already beginning to doubt the wisdom of having sacked his coachman-handyman at a minute's notice. Albert Clayton had refused—with no veneer of politeness or diplomacy—to drive his master to see his lawyer.

Brittlebank was already beginning to reflect what a large establishment Walderslow Hall was.

Charlotte Machin wondered if she would die of exposure, as had happened to a foolhardy young man a few years ago, when he had been caught in an unexpected spring blizzard while trying to march by compass from Flash to Wildboarclough. Already she had lost track of her extremities. Her ears, hands and toes were in agony to the marrow. Her ribs were trembling and she had to clench her jaw to keep her teeth from rattling. She was also oddly suprised at how *wet* a hill-mist was. It seemed to penetrate the pores of her clothing more quickly and more thoroughly than heavy rain would have done. Moreover, her hunger had intensified, and her digestive system was in turmoil.

She did not believe that she could survive this disaster, and ready though she felt in some respects to die, in others she was not. Religiously, Charlotte Machin was a woman of simplistic but firm beliefs, and although in the normal routines of her life these lay dormant and unobtrusive, they loomed terrifyingly at moments like the present.

Charlotte Machin believed that she was going to die and death, she had been authoritatively taught, was to be followed by judgement. She was not ready for judgement. In an exposed field, somewhere in the hills above the Upper Dove Valley on the Derbyshire – Staffordshire borders, she closed her eyes and prayed. She prayed for forgiveness for a number of peccadilloes over which a God overworked by the side-issues of infinity might conceivably himself have sighed for patience.

But there was one sin so horrifying that she dared not ask for absolution. Begging forgiveness for that meant reliving it, and she shied away from that, even now. At the unbidden memory of it she pushed herself up on her elbows in the wet grass, leaned over sideways and was sick.

'There's only one kind of illumination,' Ted Milward said, 'that will pierce a fog like this—the only thing that can cut a Manchester pea-souper.'

'And that is—?'

'A naphthalene flare.'

'And where in Walderslow—?'

'No hope,' Milward said. 'But I've still got a dab or two

of tar left over from when I did the henhouse. We can dip an old branch in that, and you'll have a torch of sorts. It wouldn't last long enough to get you over the hills, but it would see you across the village, perhaps even as far as the Hall.'

Brunt considered it.

'If I creep through the village trailing one hand against the walls, at least no one will see what I'm wearing.'

His clothes were still not fit to put on, though Bessie Milward had promised to do her best with them. They were soaked through, caked in filth—and stank to a degree that one would not want to take into any company.

Nevertheless, Brunt let Milward make him a torch, and with the tar-smoke acrid in his throat he set out across Walderslow. He would try to get to the Hall as soon as he could—there was the news about Barnard to be broken—but he did not want to delay a peremptory word with Harlow first.

Many pairs of eyes must have seen him pass windows. He had decided that he was going to apologize to no one for his sartorial state, not even to try to account for it. Think what they liked, people must assume that he felt nothing abnormal about himself.

Harlow and Topliss were downstairs in the bar, drinking brandy and hot water, and with the roulette wheel spinning between them on a table. Harlow was keeping a complex record of the fall of the numbers and the return on an imaginary stake.

'They're not playing for money, Mr Brunt,' Joe Bramwell hastened to explain.

But Brunt was more interested in Albert Clayton, who had somehow made his way from the Hall after his dismissal. Clearly he had been leading off against Brittlebank without restraint.

'If he thinks I'm going to drive him to Buxton on a day like this—'

Then he passed on the news that Ada Harrison had so far failed to turn up.

Then he told them that Charlotte Machin was missing.

CHAPTER 9

Harvey Harlow rose as if guiltily from the roulette wheel when he saw Brunt come in.

'Off duty, the mind needs to relax, Inspector. There is an apocryphal story about how John the Baptist once met a bowman—'

Brunt turned his head away abruptly enough to show impatient lack of interest. Nor did he make any comment on the news that Albert Clayton had just announced, but simply indicated with a jerk of his head that he wanted Clayton out of the way. The coachman made no effort to argue his rights, but finished his drink in a draught and departed.

'I must say I am relieved to see you still here,' Brunt said to Harlow.

'That is precisely what I said to our medical friend when I saw the state of the weather this morning. "Inspector Brunt," I said, "will be relieved that we are not able to take advantage of the Midland Railway this morning."'

'At least you are honest about it.'

'As I hope I am about all things. Is there any point in being otherwise?'

'Aren't you afraid I shall take your frankness as admitting some sort of guilt?'

'Why should I? I am a busy man and have more than one case in midstream in London, since I am in the vulgar condition of having my living to earn. I do not deny that having to stay and assist you in Walderslow—which I would do with alacrity, of course, if you were to ask—would nevertheless be a nuisance.'

Harlow had taken over the stance and tone of a man pontificating from a club hearth.

'I don't know how well you are acquainted with the Holmes saga, Inspector? Perhaps you recall *The Boscombe Valley Mystery,* in which a young man naïvely says he is not surprised at being arrested. Holmes, unlike the police officer concerned, construes this as a symptom of innocence.'

'Do you think we might put Holmes out of our mind for the moment?' Brunt said. 'And concentrate on the earthy realities of the Upper Dove Valley?'

Harlow smiled in conciliatory fashion.

'But of course, Inspector.'

'In that case, may we avoid any kind of prevarication, which could only be a waste of my time, and admit as common ground that it was indeed for Barnard Brittlebank that you have been working?'

'Mr Brunt—this is wholly irregular—'

'Barnard Brittlebank is dead, Mr Harlow. He is not a pretty sight, but I am presently going to take you to see him.'

Harlow did not look shocked. He looked surprised with appropriate urbanity.

'I was going to say, Inspector, that wholly irregular as this might be, there can be no such thing between you and me as a professional irregularity.'

'Good! I am glad you feel as I do about that. So perhaps now you will confirm what I brushed upon yesterday: that the purpose of your visit here was indeed to publish the falsehood that the young man had gone to Canada.'

'That is true,' Harvey said accommodatingly. 'But it is a longer story than that.'

'Let us then draw up closer to our landlord's excellent fire, and make sure that we hold none of it back,' Brunt said.

He brought out a large black notebook bulging with slips

of paper of all shapes and sizes, its pages filled with his tight but tidy handwriting.

'My acquaintance with Barnard Brittlebank,' Harlow said, 'though neither long nor deep, fell into two phases. There was a case in London in the course of which I had to call on him, and by the time that had been resolved to everyone's satisfaction we had got to know each other well enough for me to accept a small commission on his behalf.'

'The commission to publish a lie—'

'That is, if I may say so, an unjustified leap to a conclusion,' Harlow said with some force. 'I accepted in good faith what my client told me. Brittlebank did propose to disappear for the time being. For all I know, he may indeed have intended to go to Canada.'

'Why?'

'A young lady of the locality was making unfounded claims on him. She claimed to be pregnant and insisted that he was the father of the child.'

'Who was this?'

'He declined to tell me. He insisted that I would work with a freer mind in the village if I did not know. I did precisely what he commissioned me to do: I investigated his departure and learned from Mr Jedediah Nall that the young man had mentioned to him his intention to cross the Atlantic. That is the sum total of my involvement.'

'I didn't accept that the first time you told me,' Brunt said. 'And I don't accept it now.'

Harlow looked as if he might very shortly take active offence.

'You must have your own way about that, Inspector. But your lack of trust hardly gives us a basis for a candid interchange.'

'No. It doesn't,' Brunt said, with sweet-tongued simplicity.

Topliss, saying nothing as usual, was beginning to look concerned at the direction and tone of the talk.

'You will understand, Mr Brunt, that a good deal of the work of a private detective is less colourful than the plot, say of *A Study in Scarlet* or *The Hound of the Baskervilles*. In fact, a sadly increasing proportion of my time these days has to be devoted to nothing more elevated than debt-collecting.'

'If you wouldn't mind pausing between your sentences, Mr Harlow, I can make sure of getting all this down. What debt did Barnard Brittlebank owe, and to whom?'

'A 'gambling debt, I regret to say. And it was not that he was unable to pay it. In the first instance he simply could not be bothered. And then he began to resent the frequency of the creditor's applications for payment. I fear he was a young man of a certain unfortunate arrogance—apt to take the line that his creditors ought to be grateful to have him as a client. I do not need to remind you of all people that gambling debts are not enforceable at law, but that men have been known to be socially ostracized or even physically assaulted for non-payment.'

'The name of Brittlebank's bookmaker, if you please?'

'This was not a case of a bookmaker, Mr Brunt. This was a London club wager, and I fear that without his permission I am not at liberty to divulge the name of the gentleman concerned.'

'It seems to me,' Brunt said, 'that this is reminiscent of a plot of Anthony Trollope's, which at least makes a change from Sir Arthur.'

'Mr Brunt—I must ask you to believe—'

'If you are not ready to furnish the supporting facts, it's no use your asking me to believe anything.'

Brunt put away his notebook and stood up.

'Perhaps there's enough tar-dip left on my torch to light us over to Slickensides. Come and see what someone has done to your arrogant young friend.'

Harlow looked briefly at the corpse in the shed, then kept his eyes fixed high on a spot on the wall above it. 'Doctor'

Topliss was struggling to hold back vomit. Even Septimus Durden, who had led them across his yard, did not come in to see the body again.

'Yes. That's Barnard Brittlebank.'

Brunt nodded. He did not press Harlow to say how he could be so sure, solely on the evidence of build and clothing. Brittlebank's face could surely not have been identified by anybody.

'It's unlikely you'll be able to think of leaving Walderslow today, Mr Harlow. Tomorrow's something that we can't predict. But I must ask you not to go away from Walderslow without coming to see me first.'

'Of course. I shall do nothing contrary to your wishes, Inspector—though naturally, this will be on a purely voluntary basis.'

'So far. If I find evidence that you have attempted to mislead me in any particular, then our voluntary relationship will have to be looked at afresh.'

He waited a few seconds to see whether this prompted Harlow to say anything more. But Harlow looked at him with an aggressive determination to add nothing.

Brunt went close enough to the farmhouse windows to see that the Durden family were in conference round the kitchen table. Even Humphrey was sitting with them. As he saw their fog-shrouded figures about to leave by the yard gate, Septimus came to the door, anxious to buttonhole Brunt.

'Later,' Brunt said.

'At least, I hope you'll see us back to the inn with your torch,' Harlow pleaded.

'I was just about to make the offer, Mr Harlow. I'd hate you to go away from here with the impression that we're an unchivalrous lot in these parts.'

Brunt got no answer at the front entrance to the Hall, so he went round to the kitchen, where he found Brittlebank sitting candidly disconsolate, his fire still unlit and his chin unshaven.

'I'm sorry to trouble you, Mr Brittlebank. I'm afraid I've come on a melancholy errand.'

But Brittlebank did not seem to take him in, did not wish him the time of day. If he remembered who he was, he did not acknowledge him.

'I'm afraid there's been a nasty accident.'

Surely that approach was enough to make any man apprehensive—but Brittlebank seemed to lack even that much comprehension. 'A young man has been killed in the old lead mine, Slickensides.'

Brittlebank spoke for the first time.

'I know nothing about what goes on over there. I've not had anything to do with any of those people for years.'

'I'm afraid,' Brunt said, 'that more than one person has identified this young man as your son.'

Brittlebank frowned. He appeared to be considering what Brunt was saying.

'My son's gone to Canada.'

'That's what we've been told, Mr Brittlebank. But that appears to have been a falsehood, concocted for some purpose or other. The story is complicated and I am still investigating it. I'm afraid I shall have to call on you for formal identification.'

Brittlebank did not look as if he grasped what that might entail.

'I mean when it's fit to get you up there,' Brunt said. 'Later in the day, perhaps. It would be impossible for you at this moment.'

He was trying to imagine what had gone wrong in this house.

'In the meanwhile, could you tell me anything about any distinguishing marks on your son's body—any moles, warts or birthmarks?'

Brittlebank grimaced, obviously finding this an obscene

question. Brunt had an inspiration, aimed at two targets simultaneously.

'Miss Machin would know, wouldn't she? She would have seen him in his bath ever since he was a baby.'

'She'd be bathing him still, if she had her own way,' Brittlebank said. 'She didn't want him to grow up—that's been half the trouble with her—the trouble with both of them.'

'Could I speak to Miss Machin?'

Brittlebank looked at him with eyes in which the tiny blood vessels were showing rawly red.

'I'm damned if I know where she is,' he said, in a totally different kind of tone, exasperated, washing his hands of the woman.

'You mean she isn't here?'

'Can you see her, Inspector?'

'Not in this room at this moment. But surely she doesn't spend all her time down here? Are you suggesting she is not in the house? When did you last see her?'

'Last night. At bedtime.'

'Did she seem all right?'

'She was moody. She's been in one of her moods for days.'

Brunt looked at the handful of sticks that Brittlebank had been unable to ignite in the fireplace.

'Are there no other servants on the premises, Mr Brittlebank?'

'You can see for yourself that there aren't,' Brittlebank said truculently, hating to be forced to advertise his predicament. 'Apart from Miss Machin, Clayton and my cook, there's a woman comes in three times a week for the cleaning, and one once a week to do the laundry.'

'Do you mind if I look over the house?'

'There's nothing for you to see.'

'Would you like to come round with me? To see if Miss Machin has perhaps had an accident in some odd corner?'

Brittlebank did not seem to want to move from where he

was sitting, cold and desolate, but he made no objection to Brunt's going over the place. Brunt made a quick tour from room to room, saw Brittlebank's study, whose contents could tell him much about the man, but nothing about recent happenings. Charlotte Machin's bedroom told its own story of recent and hurried departure. It was an old maid's room, but not knowing the normal contents of her wardrobe, Brunt could not tell what she had taken with her. He could see that she was a woman who kept herself fastidiously clean and neat, but she did not seem to care whether she was a decade or two behind the fashions.

'You say you have a daily cook, Mr Brittlebank?'

Brittlebank told him about Mrs Harrison, but had no idea where she lived in the village. Brunt knew that he would have no difficulty in finding her.

'Where's your man Clayton? I saw him in the village not an hour ago.'

'I've given Clayton his notice.'

'When?'

'When he refused to get the carriage out for me.'

'When was this?'

'At about nine o'clock this morning. He was late for work as usual—and insolent. Inspector—are you suggesting that a man is not within his rights to hire and dismiss what servants he wishes to?'

'I'm suggesting nothing of the kind, Mr Brittlebank. But did you know that this is not a fit day to take a carriage out? I take it you haven't been out yourself this morning?'

'How can I go out?'

Brunt must return into Walderslow to see Clayton. Clayton smarting after an angry dismissal was likely to be informative.

'I'll be back, Mr Brittlebank. I'll find out what's happened to Mrs Harrison. I expect she couldn't get out this morning, either.'

*

Ada Harrison cried. She seemed to think that Brunt, a policeman of awesome legend, had come to rebuke her for failing in her duty to Horatio Brittlebank. He told her he did not see how she could possibly have got to the Hall this morning, but she did not seem convinced that he meant what he said. Not having been to the Hall today, she was unaware that Miss Machin was not there. Brunt played it craftily, did not at first tell her of this, but concentrated on trying to find out what tensions there had been in the house in the last few days. But she was too loyal to give anything away about her employers. She seemed to think that that was an attitude the law was bound to approve of.

Horatio Brittlebank was a gentleman. Barnard was a clever young man who was going to do a lot to pull up the estate. Miss Machin was a hard-working woman. Mrs Harrison could not see how the household would ever have survived without her.

'Surely there were differences of opinion between them at times?'

Storms in teacups; no wrath that the sun ever went down on.

'But Miss Machin and Barnard? Did they not fall out from time to time?'

'No. Not since he was a little boy who did the naughty things that boys sometimes do.'

They were very fond of each other, those two. Hadn't Miss Machin been a mother to him—the only mother he had ever had?

Why, earlier this year, in the summer, when he had come home from Oxford for the last time, he had celebrated by taking his old nurse for an outing in his motor-car—a horrible, noisy, frightening thing, always going wrong—though Ada Harrison had obviously been secretly impressed by its brass lamps, its polished panels and its general air of gallantry and dash.

Barnard Brittlebank had taken Miss Machin for an outing

in his motor, and she had dressed for the occasion, looking prouder and happier than Ada Harrison had ever seen her. They had gone ranging over hills and dales, had stayed out to dine at the Rutland Arms in Bakewell and had come home late. Ada Harrison unwittingly approached poetry when she described the shadows of the trees along the drive as the headlamps came racing between them.

Mind you, Horatio Brittlebank had not cared for being left alone all those hours, and having to eat his supper on his own. Miss Machin had persuaded Mrs Harrison to work late that day so that Mr Brittlebank did not feel totally neglected.

Albert Clayton had gone back into the Pig o' Lead and was *talking off ale*, as they put it, to the two men who regularly spent their mornings there. Brunt did not have to ask many questions—none at all at first—because Clayton had already drunk more than he could afford, and his tongue was as loose as it would ever be. Within another hour he would be incoherent.

He had finished at the Hall, had told that bugger Brittlebank a thing or two about himself. What a bloody house that was. No wonder they couldn't get a servant to stay.

(This was, Brunt was later to learn from Ted Milward, a less than just accusation. A dozen years ago, Brittlebank had had a good working establishment, but with very few exceptions it had run down because hands had not been replaced when they had left for various natural reasons. It was true that Brittlebank had become more and more obsessed with economies as the years had passed, but Milward was convinced that what really influenced him was his fear of being saddled with unknown personalities who might combine in parties against him.)

All of them in that bloody house were at one another's throats all the time, and it had always been so: Miss Machin nagging Horatio; Barnard deceiving her behind her back, as he had done ever since he had learned to walk and talk. The only times Horatio had ever been on his son's side had been when he spotted that Charlotte Machin was harrying him.

'But I thought he and his old nurse were as thick as thieves,' Brunt said ingenuously. 'That's the story I've always heard.'

'You've heard wrong, then, Mr Brunt. They couldn't stand the sight of each other.'

'But didn't Barnard take Miss Machin for a long ride in his motor, not all that long ago? A sort of celebration for the sake of old times?'

'Aye—and when were we ever going to hear the last of that? In the first place, Miss Machin hadn't wanted to go. She was scared stiff by the speed he always drove at. Horatio couldn't abide the bloody motor, sulked every time the youngster came home in it; well—every time he came home in a motor-car. It was one after another; he was forever smashing them.'

'He didn't crash with Miss Machin aboard, did he?'

'No. But I still don't know what got into her to go with him. I mean, he used to pass her in the house without speaking to her. And Ada Harrison was upset because they made her stay late, and it was long after ten when they got back. And she had to walk all that way home on her own. I mean, damn it, that bloody Barnard could have driven her, couldn't he?'

If you asked Albert Clayton—and you did not have to, because you were going to be told whether you wanted to be or not—that Bloody Barnard had left because he could not stand the Bloody Machin woman. And now Horatio was forever tearing into her because it was her fault he'd gone. Clayton hated everybody at the Hall so virulently that little he said could be relied on.

The finding of the corpse last night was still not general

knowledge in Walderslow. On any normal day the news would have been round the houses by breakfast-time; there would have been no point in trying to keep it quiet. But as it was, Brunt had asked the Durdens to keep the secret till he gave the word. Somebody might give himself away by knowing already.

'Suppose I were to tell you, Albert, that someone had tried to do Barnard Brittlebank a mischief? Who'd be your most likely culprit?'

'I could recruit you a bloody army who'd do him in, Mr Brunt. Tenants he's threatened to drive off their land. Servants he's persuaded his father to sack. Men whose girls he's borrowed for a night or two. And that's in this district alone. God knows how many enemies he's made in London and those places. He hasn't it in him to treat man, woman or child decently. Why? Who's had a go at him?'

But Brunt could be a natural sphinx.

The Durdens were a troubled family. After a tumultuous night they had had a troubled morning. It was not merely that the corpse had been discovered in Slickensides, not merely that one of their members might be about to be charged, rightly or wrongly, with murder. The crisis in the existence of the Durdens was of a complexity that none of them could properly have defined. The main business of the conference round the kitchen table had undoubtedly been to decide the degree of truth that had to be told to Brunt and to coordinate the telling of it. But in the midst of it each of them was finding a new kind of truth, a realization of what their life had evolved into. They also all knew, each in a different way, that a very long phase in their existence was coming to its end. In their different fashion they were as frightened of change as Horatio Brittlebank was.

Their morning had been made worse by the series of tangents that had kept postponing Brunt's visit, thus exacerbating their suspense. It was very nearly midday—the Durdens' normal dinner-time—when Brunt finally came into their yard again, the last globules of tar bubbling and guttering at the end of his torch. The Durdens were no longer round the table, but were making some show of getting on with work in the immediate vicinity of the house. Septimus was making a desultory effort to put some order into a pile of rubbish that he had ignored for years. Humphrey was helping him—surely in itself a rarity—wheeling off bits of usable timber in a barrow. He kept coming and going into the mist. Mary Ann was collecting eggs from the unorthodox crannies in which the yard poultry laid them. Her mother had her vegetables cooking though it was doubtful when they would eat, or with what appetites.

There was a confluence of Durdens as Brunt came in at the gate. He was a man whose arrival anywhere seldom brought pleasure, standing as he did uncompromisingly for the law of the land. Transgressors stood no ultimate hope in his presence—and a large proportion of those he spoke to had something on their minds that they would prefer him not to know about. But all this was countered by other qualities in Brunt. There was about him a familiarity that could come as an unexpected comfort. He was trustworthy: admittedly devious in his tactics, but in the end-result as predictable as daylight and darkness. Even his ugliness was a source of some sort of astringency. Not many people cared to look for long into his warty face and forever weeping eyes; but even those unfortunate features seemed to carry about with them a kind of assurance.

No one showed any surprise at the comic figure he cut in Milward's clothes. Brunt appeared to have forgotten that he was wearing anything odd.

'Do you want us all together, Mr Brunt? The missus has lit the parlour fire.'

The parlours of farmhouses and working homes were little used, because people had little use for them. But they existed for reasons that went deeper than social comparability.

Occasions were few in those people's lives, but the makings of a sense of occasion had to be there for when they were wanted. The Durdens' parlour had a few good pieces of furniture in it: a rosewood chiffonier and a pair of oval-back chairs. The basic ensemble was a mid-Georgian basis, though it also acted as a showcase for the later kind of bric-à-brac popularized by the Prince Consort. The room smelled uninvitingly of dust and disuse and the flames of the coal fire were having as yet little impact on the chill.

'Well—'

Septimus Durden sat rigidly in an armchair, a new gravity lining his weatherbeaten weariness.

'I didn't think it would ever come to this, Mr Brunt—not knowing what's been going on in my own family—my own flesh and blood hiding secrets from me.'

'You're talking about Barnard Brittlebank?'

'About Mary Ann and young Brittlebank. By the time I'd heard what they were up to, things had already gone too far. And when it comes to writing him a letter—putting things on paper—'

'Maybe you've only yourself to thank for that, Septimus. Maybe you've not always been all that easy to talk to.'

'Somebody has to be the master, Mr Brunt.'

'There's more than one way of being the boss in your own home. But I'm not here to talk about that. How far did things go between those two?'

'She'll tell you. She knows she's got to.'

'And you did not know it was going on?'

'I knew they'd met—and I knew what would be going on in Brittlebank's mind, given the chance. They'd met in the fields and I gave her to understand there was to be an end of it. And I was on the lookout to have a word in his ear.'

'Which you didn't manage to do?'

'Perhaps that was a mercy.'

'What would you have done to him?'

'Talked to him.'

Durden was not inhibited from letting his eyes rest on Brunt's face.

'Well, let's be honest, Mr Brunt: I might all too easily have done him a mischief if he'd said the wrong thing. Thank God it didn't come to that. That would have complicated things even further. What I didn't know was that that wife of mine was encouraging it. Well—she'll tell you she was playing a two-faced game. You could even call it a three-faced game. The end-result was to encourage the lass. It stands to sense she didn't need all that much encouraging. Which is making it harder for her to bear now. But she'll tell you. You mustn't let her try to sidle out of it. It'll do her good to work it out of herself.'

'I'll give her every opportunity, Septimus. And is there anything else you have to tell me?'

'Nothing. I could go on speculating until my mind was spinning in small circles—'

'No point in it. Did you kill Barnard Brittlebank? I have to ask you.'

'I'll take a dying oath I didn't.'

'And do you know who did?'

'I've given up trying to guess.'

'Send Mary Ann in to me, Septimus.'

Mary Ann did not come into the room coyly. She could be impossible to handle when she was in one of her wild-cat phases, but there was never anything coy about her.

She came in and stood facing Brunt, waiting for his instructions. She had clearly been drilled in the way she was to behave and equally clearly at this moment she intended to comply.

She looked tired. The distress she had suffered would have its after-aches for a long time to come. But she had beauty, even in unhappiness—the dark beauty of a young woman whose thoughts were mostly private, with something of the savagery of the landscape in which she had been brought up. She had put on a newer and cleaner frock than she would normally have worn for collecting eggs from crannies, and a crumb of plaster from a decaying wall clung to her sleeve. A few droplets of mist glistened in her hair.

'Sit down, Mary Ann.'

She did so, in the chair in which her father had sat, stiffly and unnaturally.

'There's nothing for you to feel nervous about, Mary Ann. I have a pretty good idea what you've been through, and I'm not going to try to say anything to put that right, because I know I can't. You ran away from me yesterday morning, and it might surprise you to know that I don't blame you for that.'

She looked at him without saying anything. But it occurred to him that she would see cynically through any attempt to appease her. It was what she expected him to do, and she'd know he was only doing it for his own purposes. He adopted a brighter, practical man's approach.

'There are things that we have to talk about that are not going to be easy for either of us. So what I'm going to do, Mary Ann, is just bluster on regardless. Do you know what I mean?'

She waited. She was going to do her best not to be difficult, but it would be easy to upset her equilibrium. Brunt did not think she believed that anything useful could come of this interview.

'How long were you friends with Barnard Brittlebank?'

'Since about the middle of September.'

'And you used to meet him up and down?'

'When I could.'

'Did he take you for rides in his motor-car?'

'No. He said he would one day.'

'Did you ever meet him at the Hall?'

'No.'

'Where, then?'

'In the fields. Round about.'

'How often?'

'Once or twice a week.'

Her voice was subdued, but firm and audible.

'Evenings? Night-time?'

'Sometimes in the evening. Never at night.'

'You know why I am asking you about night-time?'

'Yes.'

Like her father, she was not afraid of looking Brunt in the
eye.

'Mary Ann, I have to ask you this. Are you going to have
a baby?'

'No.'

'Did you at any time think you were going to?'

'I wasn't sure.'

'It was possible? You could have been going to?'

'Yes.'

No hesitation.

'Did you tell Barnard Brittlebank?'

'I wrote him a letter.'

'What did he say?'

'He didn't say anything.'

Now she did pause.

'I'm not sure he ever got the letter.'

'Did you see him again after you wrote it?'

'No.'

'When did you write it?'

'About two weeks ago.'

'How did you send it? By the post?'

'My mother posted it for me.'

'She knew what was going on?'

'She told me to write it.'

'She told you what to write?'

'She told me what she would write, if it was her.'

'She wasn't angry, then?'

'She was at first. She was very angry. Then she said that
if that was the way I wanted it, it was my own life I was

playing with. And if I wrote the letter, it would give me a chance to see what he might be made of.'

'So do you know now what he was made of?'

'I don't think he ever got the letter,' she said again.

'But he went away without seeing you, didn't he? We now know that he had the rumour planted in the village that he was going all the way to Canada. Doesn't that give you something to think about, Mary Ann?'

'He never said anything about Canada to me. I don't think going away from Walderslow had anything to do with me.'

'What do you think it had to do with, then?'

'I don't know. Barnard had a lot of friends away from Walderslow.'

'Did he ever talk to you about them?'

'Sometimes.'

'Can you give me any examples? Tell me a few of the things he said about them.'

She shrugged her shoulders.

'I can't think of anything. I've forgotten their names. He just talked.'

'Did he ever talk to you about going away with him?'

'He said he would like us both to get away from Walderslow.'

'Where to?'

'Places he had been to. Italy. Rome. Venice.'

'Did you go as far as making any plans?'

'Not what you could call plans. Only talk.'

'But you thought it would all come true one day?'

'I don't know. I still think he meant every word he said.'

'*I don't know. I still think he meant every word he said.* Isn't that a contradiction? Aren't you saying you'd like to have believed him, but you couldn't be sure?'

That was when the fires of rage blazed up in her eyes. If she had been standing, she might have stamped a foot.

'I *did* believe him. He did mean every word he said. You

are the same as everybody else. You think he was bad. He
was not. He had a terrible time with his father and that
awful woman who used to be his nurse. There was nothing
for him in Walderslow. There is nothing for anyone here.'

'I have not said that he was bad. I did not know him. I
can only listen to what people tell me about him—as I am
listening to you.'

But quiet speech and a reasonable answer were not
enough to placate Mary Ann now that Brunt had unsettled
her.

'I don't know why everyone has always been against
Barnard.'

Passion was uppermost in her now. There was little
chance of a return to reason until the fury inside her was
spent.

'Your mother evidently did not think he was bad,' Brunt
said softly.

'She was tricking me. She thought she was going to show
me he *was* bad. That was why she made me write the letter.
What do you think she wanted him to say to me? I could
see her smiling to herself when there was no answer, day
after day. I hate everybody. I hate Walderslow. I hate you.'

Brunt sat silently with his eyes lowered while she stormed.

'I can't stand this so-called farm. I've got to get away
from here.'

'And you have no idea who might have killed your friend?'

'How can I know that? Any of them could have killed
him. Any of them *would* have killed him. My father swore
he would kill him.'

'I think your father has probably said that about any
number of men who are still walking the earth,' Brunt
muttered, but she evidently did not hear him.

'Tell me who you mean by *them*,' he said more loudly.

She tossed her head wildly to take in the rest of the house.

'Well, I think that will be all for now, Mary Ann. If you
would be so kind as to ask your brother to come—'

But she did not get out of her chair. The dam of her self-control broke and the tears flowed, convulsing her body beyond succour. Brunt left the room and signalled to her mother that she had better go to her. Then he asked Humphrey to come and walk with him in the yard.

It was a good idea, taking Humphrey out into the fog. Brunt told him to sit on an old tub and perched himself on another a little distance away, so that the pathologically shy young man was not oppressed by being stared at. Humphrey answered his questions more readily than he had done before, though it was in a drawl so slow as to suggest slow wits, rightly or wrongly. He must have been primed with the right answers at the family council, but that was no guarantee that he would remember them.

'When did you last see Barnard Brittlebank?'

'One day last week.'

'Where was this?'

'He looked over the gate.'

'Did you talk to him?'

'He talked to me.'

'What about?'

'He asked me which way the wind was blowing.'

'And did you tell him?'

'No. I hit him.'

'Over the gate?'

'No. I went out into the road and knocked him down.'

Surely his parents had not advised him to volunteer that gem of information?

'Steady on a minute, Humphrey. You went out into the road and knocked Barnard Brittlebank down because he asked you which way the wind was blowing?'

'That's right, Mr Brunt.'

'That doesn't seem a very neighbourly way to answer a civil question,' Brunt said.

'It's an old story. It goes back a long time, Mr Brunt.'

*

When Brunt went back into the house, Ellen Durden had succeeded in doing something with her daughter and had spirited her away to her bedroom. Brunt remarked on the girl's condition.

'I'm afraid she's going to need careful handling for a week or two.'

'She has to learn to stand on her own two feet.'

'Granted. But where there's a shoulder to lean on—'

'There's not much my shoulder can do for her while she's blaming me for it all.'

'That will pass. She's bound to at first. Your part in all this does seem to have been equivocal, to say the least.'

'I don't know what that word means.'

'Ready to jump either way.'

'That's how you have to be in this life, Mr Brunt—ready to jump either way.'

He looked at her: a small-built woman, wiry and pugnaciously independent: another of the 'conscious characters', prevalent in these hills, who survived by getting her own way about things by any means that suggested themselves. The stories told about her were legion. Septimus, for example, had the reputation of soaking up so much beer at his Saturday forenoon sessions that he could and did sleep like a corpse for the next eighteen hours—a weekly relief for all the Durdens. One Saturday, Ellen had arranged for her brother to come and repair their bedroom floor, which was crumbling with woodworm. Septimus had thrown himself on the bed after his dinner, and within seconds was insensible. Then she and her brother, working together, had torn up the flooring, dragging the bed across the room as required, and, working all round it, had hammered new timbers to the joists. Septimus had not wakened until Sunday morning. His wife was a woman who took advantage of what opportunities offered.

'Did you really believe that anything good could develop between Barnard Brittlebank and your daughter, Mrs Durden?'

'Yes, I did believe that. I was wrong about it, wasn't I?' she said, setting her chin. 'Other girls have crossed that barrier. And any lass reared at Slickensides deserves a shot at any target that comes up. My Mary Ann could match up to the Brittlebanks any day of the week.'

'I don't doubt it. But you'd heard the same stories about Barnard as everybody else had.'

'Who cares for stories? They tell stories about me, too. Oh, yes—he'd been a young hellion when he was a boy. But he'd grown up, Mr Brunt. He'd been educated. He was very nice to me.'

'When? Where? What chance had he to be nice to you?'

'Since he came home. Since he'd finished his schooling.'

'How did you come across him? Here at Slickensides?'

'No: at the Hall. I've done the Monday wash there for years—a five o'clock start in the outside laundry.'

'I didn't know that.'

'You don't know everything, Mr Brunt. Every penny has counted in my time. There were some years when I didn't think we'd be able to keep Slickensides.'

'And young Barnard turned on all his charm when he happened across you? Because by then he'd spotted what Mary Ann had grown into?'

'I can see that now. I ought to have seen it from the start. I suppose I must have more than half thought that that's how it was. But I gave him the benefit of the doubt—then changed my mind. Is that what you meant by that word you used?'

'Equivocal? More or less. And what brought about your change of mind?'

'Ask Miss Machin. If you want to get at the real colour of Barnard Brittlebank, ask his old nurse. I can keep my eyes and ears open.'

'When people talk in riddles, it's usually because they have nothing to say. So something you overheard made you think that the leopard hadn't changed his spots after all? So you made Mary Ann write her letter? To force the issue? Because you knew by then that he would ditch her?'

'It made sense. The damage was done. The risk had been taken. I thought she might be pregnant. I saw no point in prolonging heartbreak, Mr Brunt.'

Brunt had been conducting the dialogue casually enough, but he seemed at this moment to be suffused with new life, as if he had suddenly found a new interest in the case.

'When did you post that letter for your daughter, Mrs Durden?'

'Two weeks ago yesterday.'

'Yes. That's what she told me.'

His torch was burned out now, and brushing his shoulder against walls and stubbing his toes against kerbs, Brunt made his way up to the Pig o' Lead. Half a dozen Walderslow men were now gathered round the roulette wheel and Harlow, acting obviously as croupier, had marked a grid of numbers on a table-top with chalk.

'Strictly for amusement only, Inspector—paper stakes only.'

Brunt ignored that and beckoned Harlow into a corner.

'This is important, Harlow. I want a true answer. I don't want to have to come and ask you again after I've checked up. When did you have your dealings with Barnard Brittlebank in London? When did he brief you to tell the Canada story?'

'I can tell you the exact date from my journal, which is upstairs. It was round about the middle of August.'

A good deal longer than two weeks ago: before Brittlebank had started anything with Mary Ann.

CHAPTER 10

Groping his way again through the choking air of the village street, Brunt walked into a milk-churn and knocked his knee-cap so badly that for seconds he thought he had crippled himself. He had to go to the Milwards', had to get out of the comic clothes he was wearing.

Bessie had his own things ready for him and he went upstairs to put them on, sat on the bed with his notebook and started making a list of the items that he had to transmit to his headquarters as soon as he could reach the railway telegraph.

> *Inform re finding body—*
> *Coroner's officer—*
> *Post mortem called for—*
> *Reports from London re Harlow and Topliss—*
> *Reinforcements—*
> *Lights—*

At about three o'clock he looked up and out of the window. The back of Milward's house overlooked a hillside on which the limbs of a sycamore some seventy yards away were beginning to loom spectrally out of the mist. It was possible now to make out the shed at the bottom of the garden. Ted Milward's forecast was coming true. An hour of semi-visibility was going to be restored to Walderslow between now and sunset. Brunt had to make his mind up about his priorities. One essential—and not the most enchanting of the jobs ahead—was to transport Horatio Brittlebank to Slickensides to identify his son. But that would simply have to wait a little longer. It was more important that Brunt should make a report to his office, so that supporting strength could be mobilized. Then there would have to be a search for Charlotte Machin, in case she had gone astray in trying to leave Walderslow on foot. He asked a very willing Ted Milward to occupy himself with that, recruiting a posse of such local men as could be relied on.

Then he set out for Parsley Hay, staying on the roads because the fields were sodden with precipitation, and there were still dense banks of sporadic vapour in which it would be possible to waste badly needed time.

It was a long message that had to be sent, and twice it had to be interrupted for railway business. Brunt asked what passengers had boarded trains today.

Trains? It had been a day of fog signals detonating on the line, of late running and cancellations. No passenger bearing any resemblance to Charlotte Machin had appeared at Parsley Hay today. The signalman telegraphed for him to other stations both ways along the line, but there was no news of her from any of them.

Brunt drank stiffly strong tea in the porters' room. He was popular on railway stations.

'Well—what's it going to do? Another day like this tomorrow?'

A wizened old porter, who looked too crooked with arthritis ever to pick up a passenger's bag, went to the door and sagely examined the sky. But there was nothing to examine. Already the sun was going down behind the now attenuated mist. There was no horizon. A haze hung amorphously round the red lantern of the station signal. The parting of the ways between the Cromford and Ashbourne lines was as far as one could see—and it was easier to make that out if one already knew what was there.

'It'll be night-dark in twenty minutes. I don't think the fog will come down really bad again much before midnight. But it'll be back.'

Brunt made a decision. He had to settle what he had to leave undone; the worst fear that had been influencing him all day was that of being cut off from Walderslow.

'Have you a lamp I could borrow? My torch battery is on its last legs.'

They found a lantern in the lamp-room and topped up the oil for him. He set out along the road again, on his way to Sterndale Cross and William Cartledge.

The vapours were also thinning around Charlotte Machin, but she was by now so hungry, cold and panic-stricken that she was hallucinating. She did not know continuously where she was or how she came to be there. And when recent events came disjointedly back to her, she lost her grasp of them again immediately in her disorder of miseries.

Then she saw that there was a drystone wall within yards of where she was lying. Where there was a wall, there was a line that could be followed. If you were in a field and knew where the wall was, then you had a way out of that field.

The bulky figures of two men took shape in front of her, and in the jerky confusion of her brain she thought that they were the two from the quarries whom she had been frightened of passing along the road this morning. She began to run headlong away from them, fell forwards and flat within very few yards. Ted Milward ran to help her to her feet.

'Miss Machin—you must have wandered off the road.'

She screamed at the man to leave her alone.

'Whatever's the matter, Miss Machin? Don't you know me? PC Milward, I used to be. Steady on, now. Take your time. We must get you back to Walderslow Hall.'

'No! Not there! Not the Hall!'

There was a large hanging oil-lamp burning in the single classroom of Sterndale Cross Church of England School. Brunt saw it gratefully from a distance, a warm yellow beacon as he came into Sterndale Cross's single street.

William Cartledge was working after hours. The children

had gone home and he was preparing a frieze of the cardinal numbers to fix to the wall. He was a young man of the same age as Humphrey Durden, slimly built, greyly and neatly but not newly clothed and with his hair closely trimmed. He had never met Brunt, but there was no one in any of these villages who did not know the Inspector by description and repute. Brunt introduced himself. Cartledge looked surprised to see him—and concerned.

'When did you last hear any news from Walderslow, Mr Cartledge?'

Cartledge looked sad—and resigned to the grounds for his sadness.

'Perhaps you'll have heard that I have good reason to want to put the place out of my mind, Mr Brunt?'

'Yes. I've heard something about that. It's not for me to express opinions—except that the story may not be over yet. I have to tell you that a man whom we believe to be Barnard Brittlebank has been found dead in Slickensides.'

'A man you *believe* to be Barnard? Surely there are enough people in Walderslow who knew him?'

'Not in the state in which we found him, I fear.'

William Cartledge looked solemn.

'When was this?'

'We found him in the middle of last night. We think he had been down there a day or two.'

'What on earth was he doing in Slickensides?'

'We can only theorize about that. Do you know the expression *nicking a man's stowe*, Mr Cartledge?'

'Yes. It's a term the miners used to use. It means—'

'We think that Brittlebank has been nicking Septimus Durden's stowe.'

'Doesn't Slickensides belong to the Brittlebanks now, though? I heard that they did a deal over Middle Furlong.'

'That is true. Horatio Brittlebank now owns the mineral rights. But the mine is still Durden's unless and until the Barmote decrees otherwise.'

'What does Brittlebank want with a mine?'

'I was hoping that you might be able to tell me that.'

'I haven't been in Barnard's confidence for years, particularly since—'

'Didn't you once go down the waterswallow with him and Humphrey when you were boys?'

'We did. The day is engraved in my memory. I was estranged from my parents for a week afterwards, because I'd been deceitful. We still don't talk about it at home.'

'Why did you go there?'

'Boyish curiosity. You might say we dared each other—but we didn't crystallize it out into those words. We didn't read that kind of schoolboy story. But what boy could stay away from a place like that—after all that Humphrey had told us about it?'

'Tell me what happened.'

'It was a day I still wish I could forget. Barnard was at his most obnoxious. He could be obnoxious in the extreme.'

Was Cartledge forgetting that he ought to be speaking well of the dead? Perhaps the fact about Brittlebank had not properly registered on him yet.

'He was not one of our friends. But if he ever joined in one of our up-against-the-wall cricket games, or came rambling over the hills, we didn't know enough about life to stand on social ceremony. But that day down the mine he showed off more than I'd ever known him show off before. The clothes he wore, the lamp he had, the way he spoke, the things he knew about, the school he was going to that autumn—he was poking fun at us all the time, letting us know how much better than us he was.'

Cartledge picked up his pen and as if unconsciously started shading in one of the numbers he was printing.

'Humphrey had been boasting, in the same way as his father always did—and in the same phrases—about the treasure that the Durdens had down there. When we pressed him about it, we soon got it out of him that it wasn't chests

of gold he was talking about. It was the makings of a
show-cave that he and his father were going to open up one
day, when they had made it safe for the public. Perhaps you
know all about that already, Mr Brunt?'

Brunt simply signalled to him to go on.

'We went down the hole. I can't say I enjoyed the experience. Perhaps I have too much imagination for that sort of
pastime, but it didn't turn out as difficult as I'd thought.
Give or take a sharp corner or two, that waterswallow is the
right size and shape to draw yourself up or down it with
your feet and elbows, while you support yourself against the
sides with your shoulders and bottom: what the climbing
experts call chimneying. We chimneyed down and we were
surprised at what we found there. It was the first inkling
that Barnard and I had had that there was any connection
between the waterswallow and the Durdens' creamery. And
beyond a bank at the bottom of the chimney there was a
passage that looked as if it led away for miles. Humphrey
said that there was a series of huge caverns along there that
he was going to show us.'

Cartledge put his pen down, as if to save himself from the
apparent rudeness of appearing to want to get on with his
work while he was talking.

'But Barnard still went on showing off. He said he wanted
to survey the place scientifically and note down exact angles
and distances: it was all part of his act, his endless exhibition-
ism. He had a small prismatic compass with him—it seemed
that one of his uncles had taught him to do some elementary
surveying on the estate with it. He handed it to Humphrey
and told him to go to the bottom of a flight of stone steps
we could see, and take a back bearing to where we were
standing: only, you understand, because he knew Humphrey
wouldn't have the first idea what he was talking about.
Humphrey just looked at the thing. He'd never seen a
compass in his life before, hadn't the faintest notion what it
was.

'"Don't you know what it is?" Barnard asked him.'

'"Of course I do. It tells you which way the wind's blowing."'

'Barnard laughed like a cackling fool.

'"You dunderhead, Durden! Dunderhead Durden! How could it possibly do that down here?"'

'We village boys, you know, didn't like being called just by our surnames. That alone was enough to get our goat. And Humphrey made matters worse. He had to try to justify himself.

'"Well, it has the same letters on it as there are on the church steeple," he said.

'I don't know how well you know Humphrey, Mr Brunt. There's more to him than you'd think. He isn't mentally backward, however he might seem. He's slow, but give him time, and he'll get there—unless it's something that he just doesn't know. But he's also quick-tempered. He'd had all he could stand of Barnard for one afternoon, and he flung the compass at his head. It missed him and struck against an area of that densely compacted rock that the mine's named after: slickensides. It went off like a pistol shot, and we were lucky, I suppose, that there wasn't a major explosion. I think it must have done no more than chip the surface. Of course, the compass was ruined, Barnard was infuriated, and he called Humphrey a club-footed oaf, so Humphrey started laying into him. Barnard wasn't big enough to be any sort of match for him—he was several years younger. I did my best to try to part them, but I'm no fighting man, and I never was a fighting boy. I did get between them, but then Barnard started in again, played dirty, and kicked Humphrey unexpectedly behind his knees. That sent him sprawling and he fell with his spine against a protruding rock. That's how he came to be hurt: something that not one of us ever admitted to this day. We said he'd slipped. His father punished him crudely and cruelly.'

'Yes. I know that part of it,' Brunt said. 'And now I understand why young Brittlebank shouted after Humphrey Durden the other day to ask him which way the wind was blowing.'

'I can imagine. Did Humphrey floor him for it?'

'So he says.'

'Well. That's the last we really had to do with Barnard Brittlebank. He went off to his public school very shortly after that, and when he came home on holiday we kept out of his way.'

It was an overcrowded, ancient-smelling little room, in which Cartledge, without assistance, taught a dozen village children, aged from 5 to 14. In the front row were three small infant desks. The young ones had a sand-tray and there were grubby clay models on a side-table. Cartledge's Civil Service Cursive Script on the blackboard taught up-and-coming Sterndale Cross a warning for life:

Know a man by the company he keeps.

The room bore the imprint of Cartledge's character: his earnestness, his consistency—and his limitations. It was the classroom of a teacher who believed fervently in his work. South America seemed to be the main interest of the current term: the elephant's-head map was pinned to a wall and beneath it photographs cut from periodicals—a pair of grazing llamas, an Aztec pyramid, an Andes mountain-scape. Yet, short of a war, few of these pupils would ever sleep more than ten miles from Sterndale Cross. A crook-handled cane hung on a hook, for all to look at all day long. Brunt wondered how much use Cartledge made of it.

'There's a question that I have to ask you, Mr Cartledge, that I am asking everyone. Did you kill Barnard Brittlebank?'

Cartledge blushed: but that did not make him guilty.

'I must, I suppose, be pretty high on your list, Inspector.

Of course, I assure you I had nothing to do with it. If you can tell me when this happened, I am sure I can account for my activities to your satisfaction.'

'I cannot yet say when it happened—but if you would go over the evenings of last week, as a matter of form—'

A choir practice, a meeting of the Parochial Church Council, a game of chess with a Merchant Navy Captain who had settled in the hamlet—

Cartledge smiled artificially.

'Would you also like a statement of my compelling motives for murder?'

'If you think they might help to exonerate you.'

Cartledge did not appear to notice the irony.

'They must have occurred to you. You must know I have nothing but contempt for Barnard Brittlebank.'

'I can understand that you feel bitter.'

'It was worse than you might think, Inspector. It was a beautiful summer evening: Barnard Brittlebank had been back in Walderslow less than a month: he did not return immediately when he came down from Oxford. I was walking over Walderslow Moor, the way I did a couple of evenings a week, to have supper with the Durdens and perhaps take a walk with Mary Ann along the Pilsbury bridle-path. And I saw them lying together, Brittlebank and Mary Ann, in a hollow. I would not have seen them if I had not left the footpath to try to see a curlew that was calling. I don't have to tell you what they were doing, Mr Brunt. There could be no doubt about it—they were writhing like animals. There was nothing barred between them. I'd never seen anyone doing it before.'

The memory of it was overheating him. His speech was at odds with his respiration as he told it.

'She was totally abandoned. There was an understanding between us, Mr Brunt, but I had never done more than kiss her or hold her hand. I could hardly believe that this was Mary Ann. She was so naturally chaste. We had talked about this: we both believed in waiting for things to happen in the proper way at the proper time.'

Propriety: William Cartledge was not a prig. He was the product of a protected corner of a society that did not question its disciplines. Moral rectitude was the charted course of civilized man. It was never a burden to Cartledge; a certainty, rather, which comforted him.

'I realize, of course, that something about Brittlebank had made Mary Ann run away with herself.'

'Did you confront either of them?'

'I was tempted to—for my wild satisfaction. But what good would it have served? It was not a question of forgiving, Mr Brunt. I could never face Mary Ann again. She can never be the same person as she was. I wrote her a short note—I wrote her, in fact, notes long and short, and many long letters, but I burned them all except the one I sent. I simply said that I had learned that she had broadened her horizons and that in the circumstances there did not seem to be any point in my coming to Walderslow again. She must have agreed with me, because she did not reply—and I have not been over there since that day. I expect the pair of them had a good laugh about me.'

Brunt sat weak-eyed and placid.

'You did not feel like competing with Barnard Brittlebank?' he asked finally.

'I never looked on him as a competitor. We do not play the same games.'

'No. I think that is probably very true.'

'I don't know what Mary Ann thought that Brittlebank was likely to offer her. I fail in all respects to understand her.'

'Well, Barnard Brittlebank seems to have understood her,' Brunt said, with a new briskness. 'And there is one more question that I am putting to everyone. As a purely personal opinion, who do you think is most likely to have murdered him?'

Cartledge looked helpless.

'Inspector—you shouldn't ask me that. How can I know? How could any answer I gave you be fair? I haven't had time to think about it. It's only in the last few minutes that I've even known. Of course, I can make guesses. But there are no grounds for them, and I dare say they would be the same as your own—except that I have not had the chance to consider the facts.'

Brunt walked back to Walderslow, an unhurried trudge that took him three-quarters of an hour. He was very tired indeed and had to force one leg in front of the other. More and more frequently these days he took pleasure in picturing the fireside of retirement.

Lights were still burning up and downstairs in the Milwards' home. Bessie seemed to be more active about household tasks than Brunt would have expected her to be at this time of day. She had brought down sheets and blankets, and seemed to be making up a bed on a sofa.

'I'm sleeping down here,' Ted Milward explained, and told Brunt that he had found Charlotte Machin in a field and brought her here.

'Physical and nervous collapse,' he said. 'It was impossible to get anything out of her, except that she would not go back to Walderslow Hall at any cost. Her mind's running over her past life in overlapping circles. It's all terribly real to her. You can see she's suffering. She keeps talking about a bathroom, among other things—keeps coming back to that bathroom. Obviously it goes back to when Barnard Brittlebank was a boy. But it's all so vivid to her. I mean, the way she was going on, I could see it myself, the steam from the bath water. I could smell carbolic soap.'

Milward padded across the room in his spreading stockinged feet to help his wife with the bedding.

'I got Dr Hamlin in and he gave her a bromide. He said that was all the help he could give her until she was thoroughly thawed out and rested. He'll be round again first thing tomorrow.'

Bessie Milward went upstairs for something else—pillows, probably—treading with cautious quietness.

'It beats me how women know these things about each other,' Milward said, putting a forefinger to his lip while she was out of the room. 'But it's amazing how often they're right. Bessie swears Charlotte Machin is pregnant. I think we've a lot to learn tomorrow.'

CHAPTER 11

The next morning dawned through a blanket even denser than the previous day's. Even in the heart of the village, visibility was less than two yards. Moreover, there was something asphyxiating in the air that did not belong to the countryside—as if the thick white atmosphere had drawn into itself months and years of the thick-textured smoke belched out by the quarry kilns at Hindlow. Yet by some quirkiness of humanity, men seemed less inclined to stay indoors than they had been yesterday. Many braved the blindfold conditions, bumped into walls and each other, felt their way about the street with their hands trailing along the stone. Others followed Brunt's example and made themselves torches with anything handy that would blaze in the open air: rags dipped in grease and carried in cleft sticks, cudgels soaked in paraffin and held aloft. Either they were ashamed of yesterday's idleness, or today's deterioration was a challenge that they were too manly to ignore.

There were scrapes and accidents. Some men's instinct, once they had taken to the road, was to barge ahead as if in the belief that it was all a matter of arithmetic, and the less time their journey took them, the less risk they ran of broken noses and limbs. The quarry workers formed themselves into a defiant band and marched out of Walderslow under triumphant brands of tallow—which had vanished from the public sight before they had gone many yards. Dr Hamlin, whose practice took him over a wide radius, was one of Walderslow's pioneer motorists and his Panhard, imported at notorious expense from France, coughed bronchially as he swung its starting-handle. And Harry Barnes, rag-and-bone man, harnessed his scrawny mare Polly for an early start to Longnor.

Barnes was not one of those who had applied any ingenuity to the subject of illumination and was making do with two cracked-dialled brougham lamps that he had himself acquired in his way of trade. His safety depended primarily on Polly's hooves making themselves heard at a distance. But their clatter could not penetrate beyond the labouring of the overworked petrol-engine behind which a detective-sergeant and two constables were driving up on secondment from Buxton. They were HQ's response to Brunt's railway telegraph messages. Their brief was to put themselves under Brunt's orders, and to deliver a sealed edict from a very high-ranking desk about the policies by which Brunt was to be guided. They had also, at Brunt's request, amassed a miscellany of lamps, burners and lanterns, including naphthalene flares. This metallically rattling rescue squad met Harry Barnes and Polly headlong not far from the spot where Charlotte Machin had strayed off the road.

The policemen had electric headlamps that sent cones of yellow light stabbing through the vapours for a distance of at least seven feet. Harry Barnes's cracked carriage-lamps threw their sorry signal about the same number of inches. Sergeant Gutteridge, who would allow no one but himself the pleasure of the wheel, braked hard. Polly shied and put a hoof-iron through the offside electric headlamp. Then she fell sideways, breaking a shaft and tipping the cart, which scattered its rags and bones over the road. Sergeant Gutter-

idge reversed to give the fallen horse space and drove his
nearside rear wheel over the edge of a ditch.

There was no need for Dr Hamlin to bring the Panhard the
short distance to the Milwards'— but the call was the first
of his circuit. Hamlin was a no longer a young man; he
achieved more by bedside astringency than by prescribing
medicine, his method being frankly to incite his patients to
cure themselves from their inner resources. He spent a long
time with Charlotte Machin and when he came downstairs
again, Brunt was waiting in ambush.

'A woman with problems,' Hamlin said. 'Which no one
can solve but herself. We've yet to see how she'll shape up.
I've treated her for minor ailments for years, and she's never
been over-anxious to help herself. She's lucky to have fallen
into Bessie Milward's hands: there's no better nurse in
Walderslow—and you two men had better keep out of their
way.'

'Can you find time to look at a body for me?'

'A body? A dead one? If it's already dead there can't be
any hurry, can there? There's an old lady at Glutton that I
must see within the next hour.'

He promised to examine Barnard Brittlebank that afternoon.

Brunt had been behaving oddly—so oddly that Bessie
had become concerned about him. And Ted, who could not
say that he knew Brunt well—indeed, who could?—was
able to give her no advice more acceptable than to leave the
man to his own devices. Bessie Milward did not like leaving
people to their own devices; she preferred to see herself
doing something for them. Luckily, there was plenty for her
to see herself doing for Charlotte Machin.

For an hour and a half before Dr Hamlin came, and for
an hour after he left, Brunt did nothing but sit at the
Milwards' front window and look mournfully out into the
fog, as if he were expecting something vital to materialize

out of it—or as if he fervently believed that the impenetrable white cloud contained some secret that would help him to interpret the teeming disorder in his brain. Now and then he brought out his bulky black notebook, sought out something he had written a few pages back and studied it as if it contained surprises. Once he took a pencil from his pocket and wrote something on a new page. When either of the Milwards spoke to him, he failed to hear them the first time. They went about their business and ceased to pay attention to him. At about eleven o'clock he put on his hat and overcoat and shuffled over to Slickensides. Bessie was relieved to see him leave her house. She went up to Miss Machin with a mid-morning bowl of broth.

Another host who was irritated to have mid-morning guests idling about his place was Joe Bramwell, whose patience was strained as he waited to clear Harvey Harlow's leisurely breakfast-table. There was something different about Harlow and Topliss today. The roulette wheel had been put away and Harlow was reading *The Last Galley*, the latest publication from the pen of Doyle. And Topliss was deeply absorbed in a racing periodical so old that its paper was yellowing and brittle. Up in their bedroom their bags were packed, except for a few things to go in at the last minute. The curious thing about the pair this morning was that they were no longer irascible about their incarceration here. They seemed resigned to it.

'We've got to let it clearly be seen,' Bramwell heard Harlow say to his assistant, 'that we don't mind. We're not put out. We have nothing to fear. If we look jumpy, it will not take Brunt long to conclude that we have reason to be.'

Ada Harrison was another of those who did better than yesterday under today's adverse conditions. Admittedly she set out early, but she did reach Walderslow Hall little more than half an hour later than her usual time. That was due to her husband, one of Brindley's day-labourers, who was prepared to lose a quarter of a day's work and pay to escort her and come for her this evening if the mists had not cleared by then. There was neither chivalry nor a sense of duty behind this. Billy Harrison could think of no other way to protect himself against his wife's maddening repetitions. If she examined her conscience again in his presence—if she went again over her reasons for turning back on the road yesterday—he believed that something in his head would crack under the strain.

Another to have had a change of heart, after loud proclamations in front of witnesses that he never would, was Albert Clayton, who had oblique reasons for going to plead with Horatio Brittlebank to give him his job back. Certain advantages accrued from being in Brittlebank's employ—rewards that Brittlebank did not even guess at. They had to do with bulk orders for fodder, fuel and various useful sundries that Clayton was authorized to make on his master's behalf, and that his master had years ago ceased to examine on delivery. The unconsidered trifles that Clayton managed to cream off from stock had become an essential part of his personal economy—and filled many a want up and down the village.

Clayton and the Harrisons met along the road: Clayton with pitch flaming at the end of an elm-branch, the Harrisons with two stable-lanterns that Brindley did not know he had lent them, and which they were swinging low, close to the edge of the verge. Thus the three of them arrived at the Hall together, prepared, if their reception was adverse, to retire at once to their homes, never to return. But that was not how things worked out. They found Brittlebank subdued, vague and ready to forgive (including withdrawing Clayton's notice) provided certain services were immediately forthcoming, and that certain promises for the future were explicit. In fact, after the initial collapse of his competence yesterday, Brittlebank had, within the limits of his domestic inexperience, gone some way towards pulling himself together. He had found cold meat and other edibles in a gauze-doored safe. He had found plates and cutlery. He always had known where wine and spirits were housed. He drank more of the latter than he would have done if there had been any danger that Charlotte Machin might catch him in the act: she might not have nagged him, but she knew how to let her mind be read. He put on his Harris homespun ulster and his Rutland cap and ventured into the outdoors. But he returned after a few tens of yards along his drive with a dawning understanding of Mrs Harrison's failure to appear yesterday (though, damn it, he had thought the woman would have shown a little more spirit).

Then he found a can of Barnard's petrol, a fluid with whose inflammable potential he was not personally acquainted, and in a blaze that looked for a moment as if it might leap from the grate and consume the entire establishment, he finally had fires going in the kitchen and his study.

'You will take me to Mr Bailey's office in Buxton, Clayton, the moment conditions improve, let us hope tomorrow. Mrs Harrison, I want you to post a letter for me when you go back to the village. I hope to be going away for a short while to visit my cousin in Manchester. And you can take time off from your kitchen duties to make my bed, if you please. And Clayton—I could have sworn we had more coal in the shed than we have—'

Brittlebank's eyes screwed up in the piggy fashion that usually meant a reckoning for some culprit—but he suppressed whatever broadside he was about to fire.

'I must ask Barnard, when he returns, to start keeping a close inventory of deliveries.'

Clayton had heard the rumour that Barnard had gone to Canada. That, he thought, would give him ample time to square up stocks.

Sufficient unto the day—

*

Brunt went to the farmhouse kitchen door. Ellen Durden looked at him with emotionless eyes.

'Mrs Durden—there's just one question that's plaguing me. Are you sure that your creamery was broken into the night before you sent the report in to us?'

'When else?'

'I just wondered. Could it not perhaps have been ten days ago?'

'Do you think we wouldn't have noticed for all that time?'

'Even that's not an impossibility,' Brunt said harshly. 'The way other things are overlooked about this place. There wasn't a lot of damage done, not much to be seen, unless you were looking for it. Even I had to come and look a second time—and your husband had not even noticed that his stowe had been nicked.'

'There was broken glass outside, on the ground under the window. I cleared that up myself. And I sent Mary Ann over to tell Constable Booth at Hartington straight away.'

'Just think hard, Mrs Durden. You wouldn't have any reason, would you, for keeping this item of news to yourself for ten days—then changing your mind?'

'Why should I? What are you getting at, Mr Brunt?'

He did not answer, deliberately adding to her mounting unease.

'The dog only died once—and that was the night the window was broken. Just what have you got on your mind, Mr Brunt?'

'It doesn't matter. Just a possibility. It isn't you I came to see, anyway. It's your boy. Where is he?'

'There's nothing else he can tell you. I know that for a certainty. Why can't you leave him alone?

Humphrey was in the creamery, skimming cream.

'You or Mary Ann had better take over from him,' Brunt said uncivilly to Mrs Durden, as if he were entitled to give her orders about the work of the farm. 'He's coming with me for a little while.'

'Where are you taking him?'

'Not far.'

Her anger was now rising, and her anxiety beginning to show through. Humphrey shambled out of the door in front of Brunt and within seconds they were no longer visible from the kitchen windows.

There was a lot of horse's blood about. It was not easy to see—and nauseating to feel—how much damage had been done. But nothing seemed to be broken and the rib-cage was unpunctured. It was no more than a flesh-wound, though not a neat one. The shaft was irreparable. Sergeant Gutteridge unfeelingly pointed out to the rag-and-bone man that with his woodwork in this condition, he would have found himself in this fix sooner or later—perhaps on an open road with no other vehicle in sight.

The animal had to be freed. The cart had to be lifted on to its wheels—a manœuvre in which its proprietor made the least effort of the four of them. The policemen also did what they could to clear its grubby cargo from the highway to the verge. Then they worked together to lift their car-wheel from the ditch. Sergeant Gutteridge crossed his fingers, praying that the axle was not fractured. Then they drove on into Walderslow, at the speed of a hearse, with one of the constables walking in front, holding above his head one of the naphthalene flares they had brought for Brunt, mimicking the man who had had to walk in front of cars carrying a red flag in the early days of motoring. This was something that the sergeant was to regret very shortly afterwards, because the moment they arrived in front of Ted Milward's, where they knew Brunt was staying, the Inspector came rushing out of the house in a storm of bad temper and ordered the flame to be put out at once.

'Tonight I'm going to need every fluid ounce of fuel I can lay my hands on. Fancy frittering it away just to get a cheap laugh out of a village street!'

Sergeant Gutteridge did not try to justify himself: detective-inspectors were entitled to their idiosyncrasies. Brunt had given the Milwards a generous demonstration of his when he brought Humphrey Durden into their house. He asked him a preliminary question or two, to which Durden replied in his usual unwilling, laconic phrases.

'When was it that your creamery was broken into?'

'The night before you came.'

'You're sure of that?'

' 'Course I'm sure.'

'Couldn't it have been as long as ten days ago that the window was broken?'

'There was glass on the ground when I went into the creamery that morning.'

But he hadn't stopped to sweep it up. Humphrey was a master of the art of not seeing jobs that needed doing. Brunt stopped asking him questions and sat for a while—for a very long while—saying nothing, simply contemplating the youth. It seemed not to embarrass Humphrey. Nothing embarrassed him as much as being spoken to. Brunt took out his notebook and filled a few more lines in it. Humphrey made no movement. Brunt put his notebook away again and looked at the man, as if his assessment of him was dismal. He looked at him without speaking for twenty minutes. Ted Milward came into the room to go and get something from the kitchen, treading as prudently as he could, in case a sensitive interrogation was in progress. But Brunt did not speak while Milward was in the room. He did not speak while Milward was in the kitchen. He did not speak while Milward was crossing the room again on his way out. Bessie Milward came down the stairs, carrying a tray of dirty crockery. Brunt did not say a word to Humphrey while Bessie had them under her observation.

Then came the furore over the waste of naphthalene. Brunt blustered out of the house, vilely angry. He brought the Buxton detectives indoors with him.

'Sergeant Gutteridge, I want you to take this young man away. I want the rumour to spread around that you've taken him to Buxton Police Station. But don't take him there. I'm not ready yet to commit myself to paper about him, perhaps won't ever be. And don't make any categorical statements to anyone that he's in Buxton. We don't want to be quoted. Do you understand?'

'Yes, sir.'

'I don't want to make you drive more than you have to on a day like this. But take him to Black Dog on the Buxton road, Isaac Bowran, landlord—he'll do anything for you, if you mention my name. Just keep Humphrey Durden there till further notice.'

'Do you want me to question him?'

'You might try.'

Brunt laughed—Gutteridge did not know what about.

The sergeant motioned to Humphrey Durden to go with him. Humphrey complied without question, without looking apprehensive—or even curious.

And it seemed that other people, in other places, were reacting to the second day of fog in the same way that Walderslow was. An errand-runner came on a hardy marathon up from Ashbourne with a message from the veterinary surgeon. The Durdens' dog had died of strychnine poisoning, a massive dose administered in minced raw steak.

Brunt read with some measure of relief the message that Gutteridge had brought him: a typed transcript of a telephone call from the head of the county CID, justifying what he had already anticipated. If there was a local medical man of appropriate acumen, Brunt was to ask him to do an autopsy—bearing in mind that a specialist pathologist might be called on later, when proper communications were restored. What mattered was how long Barnard Brittlebank had been dead. The Superintendent appreciated that in all the circumstances that might not be an easy question.

After the Milwards' midday meal, Brunt announced improbably that he was going to bed. No one thought of making any comment.

'I slept badly last night. The night before, I had no sleep at all, and it looks as if that is going to happen again tonight. And since it now looks as if everything here is going according to plan, I might as well get what rest I can. I do not want to be disturbed by anyone below the rank of Superintendent.'

As he was about to put his foot on the stairs, one of the junior detectives reminded him that he had not briefed them for anything.

'There's nothing for you to do—except keep out of everybody's way until there is. I shall have a little vulgar physical labour for you tonight.'

CHAPTER 12

This afternoon's respite from the universal blindfold was less effective than yesterday's, and it did not last as long—not more than three-quarters of an hour before daylight itself was in retreat. It was no help to Brunt to have his range of visibility increased to a hundred yards: he slept through that bounty, doggedly protected by Ted Milward from the most compelling pleas for audience.

Ellen Durden was the first insistent caller. For an ugly moment it looked as if she were going to try to force her way upstairs. Then she saw the way Milward was looking at her. He was physically capable of lifting her in his bear-like arms and depositing her outside. She backed away, leaving him to deploy the other facet of his personality, that of avuncular oracle.

'What does Brunt think he's doing, taking my Humphrey off? Does he just want to be able to report he's arrested somebody?'

'He hasn't arrested him. He just wants to talk to him.'

'That's what chills my marrow. Humphrey hasn't the sense to look after himself. He's bound to keep putting his foot in it, even though he's nothing to hide. When all's said and done, it would be a howling scandal for anybody to have to stand on the trap for killing Barnard Brittlebank. When I think what I know about him! I never told you about that, did I, Ted—?'

Dr Hamlin also came in before Brunt was awake again— but raised no objection to telling his findings direct to Milward. He had cleared all the dairying equipment from the table at which Humphrey had been working this morning and had carried out his post mortem in the creamery.

'Septimus wasn't keen—but I told him if he felt all that fastidious about it, it was high time the place was scrubbed out anyway. There's no disinfectant to beat soap and water. And as for spores in the atmosphere—after what was let loose this afternoon, I'll put in an order for a couple of his cheeses myself. There ought to be a bit of bite in the next batch.'

One of the most useful side-results of his examination of the corpse was that he categorically recognized it. He had attended Barnard Brittlebank for the usual infantile complaints and was decisive about a flaw in the iris of his right eye and a pear-shaped nævus under his left shoulder-blade.

'Killed by a blow across the face with something unyielding: iron or a lump of rock. As for how long he's been dead, it's difficult to say for certain without knowing precisely the conditions in which he's been lying in state—temperature and humidity. But he's not been dead more than a day or two—certainly not for the ten days that Brunt spoke of. There's very little sign yet of putrefaction—some tainting of the abdominal skin, but no blistering so far.'

'It's ten days since he was seen leaving Walderslow,' Milward said.

'Then he must have come back again, mustn't he?' Hamlin asked sourly.

At the Pig o' Lead Harlow and Topliss sat down to an ample midday table, though they had scarcely moved a limb since their late breakfast.

'I don't think we'll linger in London,' Harlow said. 'The South of France has a lot to commend it.'

Miss Machin's morning passed with the doctor's call and Bessie Milward's regular appearances. She dozed off and on, and Bessie did all she could to foster a restful atmosphere. But Miss Machin was not restful. She was anxious to get up and go somewhere, kept talking of the coast, and Bessie's assurance that she was welcome to stay here as long as she liked seemed to bring her no comfort. She looked as if it would not take much to persuade her to talk—but for the time being Bessie discouraged her from talking. This was not primarily out of intuitive good nursing, nor was it entirely a psychological tactic. It had always been Bessie's inalienable routine that mornings were for housework until housework was done. Talk belonged to afternoons.

After she had taken Miss Machin her dinner (which Miss Machin called lunch) she took one of her pillows away from her and made her lie flat and promise to try to sleep, which she did. Bessie looked in on her once or twice during the next hour. At three o'clock she was awake again. Bessie gave her her pillow back and sat down on the edge of the bed with the air of a woman who had time to spare. The time for talking had come.

It was seven o'clock in the evening before they heard Brunt get out of bed. Milward and his wife, alone together in their living-room, exchanged a glance. Brunt asleep was considerably less strain on a household than Brunt awake.

But when Brunt reappeared, he was in a changed mood. Sleep seemed to have done him a miracle of good—and he looked as cherubic as his warts permitted. He was no longer restive. He no longer relapsed into quirky silences. He was eager to hear what messages had come in, but did not get excited about them. He asked no questions about them, did not need to have any points repeated.

'So Brittlebank must have been somewhere near enough to have come back under cover of darkness to do his stowe-nicking. I'm glad that's cleared up. It worried me. It was an anomaly. Anomalies always do worry me. From now on it should be plain sailing.'

Bessie gave Brunt his supper and went upstairs again to her patient—to whom she was now referring as Charlotte, as if they had been on first-name terms all their lives. Milward had clearly been waiting keenly for the opportunity to talk to Brunt in privacy.

'A woman with problems: that's what Doc Hamlin said about Miss Machin.'

'She's talked to Bessie, I take it?'

'It was nothing short of a confessional.'

'Unprotected by any self-imposed priestlike vows, I hope?'

'If you ask me, it's better for those about her to know the truth—even if she never guesses that they know it. Spot of rum and water, Tom?'

Brunt accepted readily, and Milward poured them a tot each.

'It's funny, you know, what will eat into people's minds —especially somebody lonely. What wouldn't matter a monkey's fart to one person will hound another into an asylum. When we first brought Miss Machin in yesterday afternoon, she was not talking hang-together sense. She knew where she was, and who I was—and yet she didn't.

All she knew for certain was that she wouldn't ever go back to the Hall. There were some things that were eating her heart out, and she kept coming back to them. She kept shouting young Brittlebank's name, as if he were a kid again and wouldn't take notice of her. And the most persistent thing was something about a bathroom. Time and time again she kept coming back to that. Well, this afternoon, she told Bessie what that was all about—as ashamed of herself as if it was highway robbery she was confessing to.'

He offered Brunt a second tot, which Brunt declined. He took another himself.

'It was when Barnard Brittlebank was eight or nine, and Charlotte Machin had been living with the family that many years, and she was bathing the boy at bedtime. She could describe the smell of the steam and the soap and the warmth of that towel from the rack. And accidentally she happened to get hold of the little lad's pinkle a bit harder than she'd meant to—and she took her hand away fast. But he said, "Do that again." You'll understand, it was nothing more than a little bud in those days—

'Well, she told Bessie, she has never known what came over her, but she did do it again, and he liked it and grinned all over his face, and then she was ashamed of herself and got him into bed as fast as she could. And after that, she began to hate bathing him. It's difficult to understand why it mattered to her as much as it did; and yet I suppose it's possible to see into her mind. She said she kept being tempted. Yet what sort of a temptation is that, to touch an eight-year-old's willy? A woman of—well, she'd be in her early twenties at the time? She swears she only did it the once, but one night, a week or two later, he asked her to do it again. She wouldn't, and was brusque with him, and Brittlebank Senior must have heard that something out of line was going on—or maybe he just sensed it. He told her the boy was growing up, and she ought to leave him more to himself at bathtime—which upset her very much indeed. I think, with her peculiar kind of conscience, she must have thought that old Brittlebank knew more than he did. God! Doesn't it shake you, the sort of thing one woman will tell another?'

Barnard took Charlotte Machin for their famous outing one day towards the end of the idle high summer. Throughout their lives, love had been obliterated by hate and exasperation, but since his return home this time he had treated her with a new respect and a hint of conspiratorial friendship. He was capable of charm and he knew how to use it to his own ends. And she, who ought to have known full well that his charm was always suspect, was nevertheless always relieved to read its signs. This was a new Barnard. His student days were over. He had evidently put his objectionable adolescence behind him—had grown up, in fact.

He spoke to her several times about an excursion in his car. Clayton's description to Brunt of her attempts to decline were tendentious exaggeration. She simply made him promise to drive moderately. And on a clear evening he drove her over the tops, down the Via Gellia to Cromford, and up alongside the splashing Wye through the Matlocks to Bakewell. He dined her sumptuously, kept her wineglasses over-generously topped, bought her a Benedictine, for which she had an almost girlish liking (and which came her way no more often than every few years).

'If you ask me,' Ted Milward said, 'he'd laced it. A gentleman once told me when I was on desk-duty at Wirksworth Station years ago, that if there's one thing guaranteed to put any woman in a loving mood, it's Benedictine laced with a drop or two of brandy.'

Barnard reminisced enchantingly about highlights they had shared: Bognor and Boulogne. He told her that the good things were not all in the past, that her real life's fun was only just beginning. She really did begin to believe that with a mature Barnard permanently home, a new phase of life was on the horizon.

She was startled to learn how late it was when the time came to leave the Rutland Arms. They drove home through Sheldon, steam hissing from the radiator-cap as they struggled up the hill. Barnard had to wait for his engine to cool and they got out and marvelled at the moonlight over Great Shacklow Wood. Still Barnard had not touched her with as much as a fingertip. It would be fatal to be repulsed too soon, and it was clear to Milward and Brunt that he had been in consummate command of what he was doing. She was conscious of his nearness, his breathing behind her head as he helped her on with her wrap. But of course she had no thoughts beyond the rarity of the evening: there were realities that she, a barely credibly sheltered woman, did not begin to understand. She was enjoying herself—and glowing from what she had drunk: more than ever in her life before.

As they parted for bed, Barnard bowed to her in a way that touched her heart. As the bedroom door closed behind her she was in a haze of outward well-being and inner contentment. Barnard timed the next sequence of events with a skill suggesting that not all his time over the last few years had been spent poring over books. When she was in her nainsook nightdress and crossing her room, finally to bed, he tapped lightly on her door in the same second as opening it. He was in a pale green figured silk dresing-gown and she thought at first that there was some household service that he had come to ask of her—a nightcap, or a request to be called in the morning. But instead he came to her and put both hands on her shoulders.

'I do thank you most sincerely, Charlotte, for all you've ever done for me—and especially for your company this evening.'

And then he let his dressing-gown fall open—not suddenly, as a man out to shock a woman, but as if it was the natural gesture that she was expecting of him.

'Mr Barnard—!'

That was what she had started calling him after he went away to Oxford.

'Oh, come, Charlotte—I'm no stranger to you, surely? Touch me *there*—like you used to when I was in the bath.'

But what she saw *there* was not what she had seen when he was eight years old. This was a monster, an instrument of ultimate atrocity.

He pushed her to the bed, snatched at the fabric of her nightdress, threw his weight over her. He was throbbing into her before she could believe the truth of what was happening. He left her with her brain aching as it sloughed off its alcoholic vertigo, physically sick, in unrelievable pain and contaminated with what she could only think of as filth.

'Rape,' Milward said. 'You can't call it seduction.'

'But in the monstrosity of it,' Brunt said, 'she would think of herself as more than half guilty.'

'Why, why, why, Tom? Why does a man do a thing like that?'

'Because Barnard Brittlebank had to put his mark on all he encountered.'

Brunt asked Milward to leave him alone for half an hour. Milward padded off to find himself something to do elsewhere in the house. Brunt then sat perfectly still, brought out his black book after five minutes and filled a page with tabulated notes at which he sat and gazed for some time. Then he put the book away and sat testing his memory, not a flicker crossing his features. The timing of events for the next few hours was crucial.

When he was satisfied that he was detail-perfect, he called his two young detectives and briefed them patiently but crisply. It was mainly a question of their entering the grounds of Slickensides Farm by one of its rear walls with the utmost quietness and helping him in with the variety of lamps and flares that Gutteridge had brought him. They were then to go to ground in nooks in the Slickensides yard and not show themselves, no matter who came down the mine after Brunt. If that person were to re-emerge unaccompanied by Brunt, then he or she must be detained, and one of them must come down the mine, ready for anything. They were both to come down if no one had come out by dawn.

The lamps and lanterns were relayed to the creamery door, whose locks Brunt picked in silence and darkness. Then he went in, removed three only of the floorboards under the stowe and took all his lighting illumination to the top of the adit, which took him five journeys.

Working at a leisurely pace, but never resting, he deployed his illumination where he wanted it, mostly near the spot at the foot of the waterswallow where Barnard Brittlebank had lain in an eight-foot pool. By the time he had finished, there was more to be seen of Slickensides than had ever been possible in the history of the mine. There was great beauty here, since Brunt could now see for the first time the rock-faces of which Septimus Durden had spoken, vividly coloured by mineral deposits carried by dripping water. Even more impressive was the sense of being in a vast, deserted and in some indefinable sense cruel place, immeasurably more ancient than man. But if Brunt was affected by æsthetic or prehistorical considerations, he did not allow them to interfere with the pattern of his work.

First he looked at the rock-face that Durden had shown him, where Humphrey had splintered a patch of slickensides when he threw Barnard Brittlebank's compass. Then he looked for slickensides in other places, traced its grooved surface down along the line of the fault to the wall opposite where the corpse had been. In no place had it ever been disturbed, and there was no predicting what violence would be released if it were.

Now Brunt clambered down through the gap where Septimus had demolished the bank, and where he had fixed the most powerful of his flares. He was looking for something, but it did not take him long to abandon the search. If the weapon used for killing Brittlebank was down there, it was now under many tons of avalanche.

Brunt came out of the mine, through the creamery, out into the yard and began to make noise. He smashed another pane in the window, kicked a pail, stamped heavily on the dairy floor—then hurried back, down the rickety ladder, down the stone steps, down the slope to the outfall of the waterswallow, where he had left all his lamps burning.

He did not have long to wait. The cavern was now flushed in so much light that the additional lantern of a newcomer made no noticeable difference. But what was striking about the new arrival was the speed and sureness of the footsteps: not picking a cautious way down the steps, no slithering on a bottom down the slope—but actually running down the gradient, with the agility of a ballet dancer, and no fear of falling. Ellen Durden jumped down beside Brunt. She was carrying a *bucker*, a broad-headed hammer of the kind that miners' women had used for breaking up ore.

'That's what he did it with, is it?'

Brunt held out his hand for it and she passed it to him, looking at him for a moment of hatred that might not stop at anything.

'Aren't you afraid, Mr Brunt?'

'You won't kill me, Ellen, for two reasons. One is that you're trapped down here with me: I have two men outside. And the other is, you'd rather I talked to your Humphrey than left him to Sergeant Gutteridge.'

'Mr Brunt—if I told you that *I* killed Barnard Brittlebank, you'd say I was only trying to save Humphrey's skin.'

Brunt contemplated her with an expression that told her nothing.

'I might believe you,' he said at last. 'But you'd have to prove to me that you knew exactly what happened—without making any mistakes. What did you do it with?'

'With the bucker. I'd picked it up, coming through the creamery. There's any amount of old tools in there.'

'Where was he when you killed him?'

She pointed to where they had found him face downwards.

'You found him where he fell.'

'Why didn't he float when the water rose?'

'I threw rocks on him.'

'Why?'

'Ashes to ashes.'

'What had brought you down after him?'

'The noise he made breaking in. It was one of those nights. Septimus had been drinking at home—drinking like a pirate. He'd drunk himself senseless. I couldn't sleep, and I heard the window break, saw his light. I pulled some clothes on and came down to have it out with him.'

'How long did it take you to get to him?'

'I was in no hurry. I gave him time. I wanted to see what he was up to.'

'And what was he up to?'

'I stood to one side of the window and watched him nick the stowe.'

'Don't you think he was taking a mad risk? He'd given himself a cover-up story to get away from Walderslow, with one, and as he thought, two women in trouble. So why come back at night like that?'

'Because he was dead set on getting Slickensides for himself. He couldn't wait to start the process. He'd have had to come back to Walderslow sooner or later. If he couldn't afford to himself, his father would have bought the women off, once things had cooled down. It happens all over the place.'

'He had no need of Slickensides.'

'We don't know what he had need of. He must have spent no end of the money his mother left him. Like that fool of a husband of mine, he saw a show-cave as income for the future. And with Barnard Brittlebank, what he wanted wasn't what he needed: what he wanted was what he saw someone else had got. You never met Barnard Brittlebank. I did, and I know the way his mind worked. Do you know what he was actually doing, when I took him by surprise down here?'

'You're supposed to be telling me.'

'He'd picked up a sharp-ended stone and was hammering at the slickensides in front of him.'

'Sounds as if he was playing with suicide.'

'No. It was the same thing as wanting the mine, the same thing as throwing tenants out of home and plot, the same thing as getting Charlotte Machin in the family way. He had to do things because they were in front of his nose. He had to be the master of everything he could see. When they were boys, the day my Humphrey got hurt, they told him about slickensides. Humphrey had thrown a compass thing at it, and they were lucky it was no more than a surface split. Brittlebank wouldn't believe them, and wanted to try it out in a big way—to prove they were wrong. Humphrey had to fight to stop him. That's how Humphrey fell and bruised his spine. And the other night, when Brittlebank came down here and saw slickensides again—there was no power on earth could stop him trying—except my bucker—'

'It's a pity you bothered. It could have saved us all a lot of trouble if you'd let him try.'

'I was too bloody close to him. I didn't want my face stove in with slickensides. Well—have I got the story right?'

'Enough. But don't you think you were taking a chance, calling me out?'

'Wasn't that the normal thing to do?'

'He could have lain down there for ever.'

'And what if you'd come looking? You did come looking, damn you. Give me a chance, Mr Brunt. I'll be up after you in three minutes' time, if it doesn't work.'

Brunt stood and thought. The unnaturally yellow light brought out a strange texture in his totally uninformative face.

'*Please*, Mr Brunt. I couldn't bear to sit on a prison bed for three weeks, listening to morning clocks striking eight.'

Brunt stood for another few seconds, then turned without speaking and began to climb the rough slope. He had reached the foot of the final ladder when the hollows below him reverberated to a crash that sounded as if it had brought the whole mine into rubble. He turned, looked down and waited. Like her son seven years ago, Ellen Durden had been lucky.

When the early morning train from Ashbourne stopped at Parsley Hay, Harlow and Topliss got into a First Class compartment. The first thing they did as the train pulled out was to divest themselves of their Baker Street garb and put it away in one of their suitcases.

Five minutes later, at Dowlow Halt, Brunt opened a Third Class door in the same carriage. There was only the lightest of mist this morning, but he paid no attention to the landscape. He kept falling asleep. Brunt was very tired indeed, beyond keeping his eyes open. He saw the quarry-smoke at Hindlow, but not the branch line to Ladmanlow. He saw Staden Moor, but not the Duke's Drive viaduct: all this over a distance of less than five miles.

At Higher Buxton he made an effort to pull himself together. On the Buxton platform, Harvey Harlow wished him good morning with exaggerated courtesy.

'Good morning, Mr Harlow.'

And as they heard the name, two men stepped out from behind a pillar.

'Mr Harlow? I must ask you to come with us.'

Because Harlow's first meeting with Barnard Brittlebank had had nothing to do with any gambling debt. It had had to do with a young lady in London who was craving compensation for a broken promise that she claimed had ruined her life. Harvey Harlow had done quite comfortably for himself with the terms that he had negotiated—and had had the bonus of an additional commission for Brittlebank.

But he had not stopped at that. Unlike Sherlock Holmes, he did not restrict himself to delivering malefactors to bumbling policemen. He took any side-chance that offered, and saw here an opportunity to blackmail a young lady with her future to consider. Unfortunately for him, she had enough spirit to complain to Scotland Yard, and under the anonymity of 'Miss X' had been persuaded to lodge charges. A man from London was on his way to talk to Harvey Harlow in Buxton today.

At the adjourned inquest, the coroner acceded to Brunt's formal request for permission to refresh himself from the pages of his black notebook.

He gave evidence—as did Septimus Durden after him—of the breaking down of the bank that let out the water and uncovered Barnard Brittlebank. His shoulders were covered with fallen rocks.

Dr Hamlin gave evidence of fatal injuries consonant with blows to the face with something unyielding: iron or a lump of rock.

A geologist from the Victoria University of Manchester gave evidence of visiting Slickensides Mine and finding that the spot where Brittlebank's body was found was scattered with calcite and bed-rock limestone, evidently thrown out by a recent explosion of slickensides. He explained the phenomenon and the jury examined his sketch of the area of the wall from which these stones had been blasted.

Ellen Durden gave evidence of following a nocturnal intruder into the mine—the coroner was later to commend her for her courage. She heard a tremendous explosion as she was about to descend the adit, and when she reached the man, he was already lying on his face, partially covered with rubble.

The verdict was Death by Misadventure. Brunt waited for the Derby train to take him home for his tea.

They said in Walderslow that it was all the Old Man's doing. More than half the drinkers in the Pig o' Lead believed this without qualification—and they would all have liked to.